TOEIC

練習測驗（4）

LISTENING TEST

In the Listening test, you will be asked to demonstrate how well you understand spoken English. The entire Listening test will last approximately 45 minutes. There are four parts, and directions are given for each part. You must mark your answers on the separate answer sheet. Do not write your answers in your test book.

PART 1

Directions: For each question in this part, you will hear four statements about a picture in your test book. When you hear the statements, you must select the one statement that best describes what you see in the picture. Then find the number of the question on your answer sheet and mark your answer. The statements will not be printed in your test book and will be spoken only one time.

Statement (C), "They're sitting at a table," is the best description of the picture, so you should select answer (C) and mark it on your answer sheet.

1.

2.

GO ON TO THE NEXT PAGE.

3.

4.

5.

6.

GO ON TO THE NEXT PAGE

PART 2

Directions: You will hear a question or statement and three responses spoken in English. They will not be printed in your test book and will be spoken only one time. Select the best response to the question or statement and mark the letter (A), (B), or (C) on your answer sheet.

7. Mark your answer on your answer sheet.

8. Mark your answer on your answer sheet.

9. Mark your answer on your answer sheet.

10. Mark your answer on your answer sheet.

11. Mark your answer on your answer sheet.

12. Mark your answer on your answer sheet.

13. Mark your answer on your answer sheet.

14. Mark your answer on your answer sheet.

15. Mark your answer on your answer sheet.

16. Mark your answer on your answer sheet.

17. Mark your answer on your answer sheet.

18. Mark your answer on your answer sheet.

19. Mark your answer on your answer sheet.

20. Mark your answer on your answer sheet.

21. Mark your answer on your answer sheet.

22. Mark your answer on your answer sheet.

23. Mark your answer on your answer sheet.

24. Mark your answer on your answer sheet.

25. Mark your answer on your answer sheet.

26. Mark your answer on your answer sheet.

27. Mark your answer on your answer sheet.

28. Mark your answer on your answer sheet.

29. Mark your answer on your answer sheet.

30. Mark your answer on your answer sheet.

31. Mark your answer on your answer sheet.

PART 3

Directions: You will hear some conversations between two people. You will be asked to answer three questions about what the speakers say in each conversation. Select the best response to each question and mark the letter (A), (B), (C), or (D) on your answer sheet. The conversation will not be printed in your test book and will be spoken only one time.

32. Why is the man calling?
   (A) To confirm the date of a performance.
   (B) To buy some concert tickets.
   (C) To change the location of his seats.
   (D) To check the status of an order.

33. What problem does the woman mention?
   (A) An account was closed.
   (B) An event was postponed.
   (C) Some tickets were not sent out.
   (D) Some shipping addresses were wrong.

34. What does the woman suggest?
   (A) Checking a Web site.
   (B) Placing another order.
   (C) Using a different credit card.
   (D) Going to the box office.

35. What does the woman want to use?
   (A) A conference room.
   (B) A swimming pool.
   (C) Cleaning supplies.
   (D) Storage space.

36. What event is the woman planning?
   (A) A birthday celebration.
   (B) A wedding.
   (C) An anniversary.
   (D) A retirement party.

37. What does the woman have to do before Friday evening?
   (A) Pay a security deposit.
   (B) Return the equipment.
   (C) Return her keys.
   (D) Pick up her mother.

38. Where most likely are the speakers?
   (A) At a department store.
   (B) At an airport.
   (C) At a bank.
   (D) At a restaurant.

39. What problem does the man mention?
   (A) He forgot his wallet.
   (B) He went to the wrong airport.
   (C) His flight was delayed.
   (D) His luggage was lost.

40. What does the woman tell the man to do?
   (A) Fill out a complaint form.
   (B) Come back later in the day.
   (C) Speak to a manager.
   (D) Go to the fourth floor.

41. Who is Les Walker?
   (A) A hotel manager.
   (B) A photographer.
   (C) A Web site designer.
   (D) A lawyer.

42. According to the man, how has the company changed over the last year?
   (A) It has a new owner.
   (B) It has more employees.
   (C) It has expanded its product line.
   (D) It has merged with another firm.

43. What is the woman concerned about?
   (A) The accuracy of a database.
   (B) The price of invitation.
   (C) The size of an event space.
   (D) The choices on a menu.

GO ON TO THE NEXT PAGE.

44. What is the woman planning to do tonight?
  (A) Leave on vacation.
  (B) Meet with a client.
  (C) See a play.
  (D) Go out for dinner.

45. What does Man A recommend?
  (A) Arriving early.
  (B) Taking a bus.
  (C) Hiring a driver.
  (D) Reserving tickets.

46. What does Man B suggest?
  (A) Taking the subway.
  (B) Leaving later.
  (C) Going with a friend.
  (D) Asking for a refund.

---

47. Where do the speakers most likely work?
  (A) At a savings bank.
  (B) At a marketing agency.
  (C) At a technology firm.
  (D) At a television station.

48. What does Maggie say about video conferencing?
  (A) It tends to be problematic.
  (B) It will enable more employees to participate.
  (C) It allows for more frequent meetings.
  (D) It makes meetings easier to schedule.

49. What does Leah mean when she says, //"I hear you loud and clear, Leah."//?
  (A) She has a different point of view from Leah.
  (B) She doesn't understand what Leah said.
  (C) She agrees with Leah's statement.
  (D) She thinks Leah is speaking too loudly.

50. Why did the woman call the department store?
  (A) To complain about a defective product.
  (B) To inquire about an annual sale.
  (C) To apply for a job.
  (D) To schedule an appointment.

51. What does the man advise the woman to do?
  (A) Contact the manufacturer.
  (B) Purchase a new machine.
  (C) Go to the store's service desk.
  (D) Extend a warranty.

52. What will the man most likely do next?
  (A) Look up some information on his computer.
  (B) Issue a full refund for the machine.
  (C) Contact his supervisor.
  (D) Transfer the woman's call.

---

53. What information does the man request?
  (A) Whether a facility is open to visitors.
  (B) Where the building is located.
  (C) Who will lead a tour.
  (D) How much tickets will cost.

54. What can visitors do at the workshop?
  (A) Observe a science experiment.
  (B) Buy some plants.
  (C) Watch a video about the laboratory's history.
  (D) Speak with some of the craftsmen.

55. What does the woman recommend?
  (A) Purchasing a ticket online.
  (B) Becoming a volunteer.
  (C) Booking a private tour.
  (D) Visiting on a weekend.

56. What will the woman use the new software for?
- (A) A Web design.
- (B) Sales figures.
- (C) Payroll.
- (D) Market research.

57. What is the problem with the software?
- (A) It does not produce required reports.
- (B) It runs very slowly.
- (C) It is difficult to install.
- (D) It is expensive.

58. What does the woman suggest?
- (A) Buying additional software.
- (B) Scheduling a training session.
- (C) Restarting a computer.
- (D) Contacting another department.

59. What does the man ask the woman to do?
- (A) Coordinate an event.
- (B) Give a lecture.
- (C) Help a patient.
- (D) Chair a committee.

60. Why might Dr. Taylor be busy on October 12?
- (A) She will be going on leave.
- (B) She will be attending a board meeting.
- (C) She will be working with interns.
- (D) She will be performing surgery.

61. What does the man offer to do?
- (A) Arrange for transportation.
- (B) Speak to a manager.
- (C) Hire an assistant.
- (D) Reschedule an event.

CHADWICK INSTITUTE OF PROFESSIONAL DEVELOPMENT

COLLEGE OF COMMUNICATIONS

Course	Code/Section	Instr.	Date/Time	
Public Speaking	COM102B	Baines, L.	MWF	0900-1100
Public Speaking	COM102C	Baines, L.	TTh	1300-1600
Public Speaking	COM102D	Garza, T.	MWF	1830-2030
Public Speaking	COM102E	Lupin, F.	Sat	0900-1530

62. What does the woman ask the man about?
- (A) Client interest in a product.
- (B) Requirements for a job promotion.
- (C) Adjustments to the work schedule.
- (D) Funding for professional development.

63. What does the woman say has recently happened at the company?
- (A) A management position was created.
- (B) An overtime policy was changed.
- (C) An agreement was reached with another company.
- (D) A retail location was closed.

64. Look at the graphic. Which course would the woman most likely take?
- (A) COM 102B.
- (B) COM 102C.
- (C) COM 102D.
- (D) COM 102E.

GO ON TO THE NEXT PAGE.

Belmonte Car Rental

CLASS
Economy Traveler Collection

Standard rate: $59.99 per day

Model*	Cap.	MPG
•Ishii Courier (or similar)	4+	43 or better
•Kramer Cruiser (or similar)	5+	36 or better
•Taris Citicar Hybrid	4+	57 or better
•Cheon Blast Wagoneer Hybrid	5-6+	46 or better

*Specific makes/models within a car class may vary in availability and features such as passenger seating, luggage capacity, equipment and mileage

65. Where does the man most likely work?
(A) At a car rental company.
(B) At an auto repair shop.
(C) At a hotel.
(D) At a travel agency.

66. Why does the woman say, "That's the thing."?
(A) She agrees with the man completely.
(B) She has found the item she was looking for.
(C) She will call back later.
(D) She will explain her situation.

67. Look at the graphic. Which vehicle will the woman most likely select?
(A) Ishii Courier.
(B) Kramer Cruiser.
(C) Taris Citicar Hybrid.
(D) Cheon Blast Wagoneer Hybrid.

TO-DO LIST

Employee Mixer, Friday, July 9

☑ Get budget approved by Mr. Timmons

☑ Buy-out Jack's Cocktail Bar

☑ Arrange for catering (finger food; pizza, maybe?

☐ Hire DJ

☐ Pay deposit at Jack's

☐ Design and print flyer announcement

☐ Send out company-wide memo

68. What does the woman want to do?
(A) Attend a training session.
(B) Meet with a colleague.
(C) Hire some entertainment.
(D) Visit an art gallery.

69. What does the man say he will send?
(A) His resume.
(B) A contract.
(C) Some references.
(D) A mixtape.

70. Look at the graphic. Which of the following tasks has the woman completed?
(A) She has posted a flyer in the employee break room.
(B) She has hired the entertainment.
(C) She has sent out an e-mail to her colleagues.
(D) She has arranged for catering.

PART 4

Directions: You will hear some talks given by a single speaker. You will be asked to answer three questions about what the speaker says in each talk. Select the best response to each question and mark the letter (A), (B), (C), or (D) on your answer sheet. The talks will not be printed in your test book and will be spoken only one time.

71. What new service is being announced?
    (A) Club membership.
    (B) Online banking.
    (C) Home delivery.
    (D) Catering.

72. What does the speaker suggest that listeners do?
    (A) Enter a contest.
    (B) Confirm an order.
    (C) Use a coupon.
    (D) Visit a website.

73. According to the speaker, what will happen this evening?
    (A) A business will close early.
    (B) A delivery will arrive.
    (C) A prizewinner will be announced.
    (D) A holiday sale will begin.

74. What is the purpose of the announcement?
    (A) To explain safety procedures.
    (B) To describe a new printer.
    (C) To share an employment opportunity.
    (D) To report an upcoming inspection.

75. What benefit does the speaker mention?
    (A) Reduced harm to the environment.
    (B) Greater flexibility with clients.
    (C) Increased worker productivity.
    (D) Fewer maintenance problems.

76. What will happen on Friday?
    (A) Some employees will be laid-off.
    (B) A printer will be delivered.
    (C) Clients will visit.
    (D) Training sessions will be held.

77. What project is the speaker discussing?
    (A) Building a garage.
    (B) Replacing some pipes.
    (C) Repairing a roof.
    (D) Remodeling a kitchen.

78. What problem does the speaker mention?
    (A) The weather will be poor.
    (B) A permit has been delayed.
    (C) A deadline cannot be met.
    (D) Some piping is not available.

79. What does the speaker offer to do?
    (A) Reduce a price.
    (B) Hire additional workers.
    (C) Refer other companies.
    (D) Discuss a project.

80. What is Votorola planning to offer?
    (A) Research grants.
    (B) Software updates.
    (C) Internet access.
    (D) Summer internships.

81. Why did Votorola choose June 5 as a start date?
    (A) To respond to a client's request.
    (B) To meet a contract deadline.
    (C) To celebrate an anniversary.
    (D) To mark a holiday.

82. What will listeners most likely hear next?
    (A) A public service announcement.
    (B) An interview with a business executive.
    (C) Answers to audience questions.
    (D) More details about the new service.

GO ON TO THE NEXT PAGE

83. What type of event is taking place?
    (A) A concert.
    (B) A grand opening.
    (C) A storewide sale.
    (D) An award ceremony.

84. What does the speaker mean by //"one car stood head and shoulders above the rest"//?
    (A) Its design was clearly superior to the others.
    (B) It is taller than all the other cars.
    (C) It resembles a human being.
    (D) It is the most reasonable of the entries.

85. What is implied about the contest?
    (A) It's for children.
    (B) It's never been held before.
    (C) It's sponsored by an elementary school.
    (D) It's held every other year.

86. Where does the speaker most likely work?
    (A) At an advertising agency.
    (B) At a sporting goods store.
    (C) At an art gallery.
    (D) At an architectural firm.

87. What does the speaker ask the listeners to do?
    (A) Submit a design.
    (B) Organize some files.
    (C) Come to work early.
    (D) Contact a client.

88. According to the speaker, what will take place over the weekend?
    (A) A client meeting.
    (B) A community event.
    (C) A ground-breaking ceremony.
    (D) A professional workshop.

89. What industry does Mr. Letovsky work in?
    (A) Architecture.
    (B) Health care.
    (C) Social media.
    (D) Finance.

90. What main accomplishment is Mr. Letovsky recognized for?
    (A) Starting a charitable organization.
    (B) Improving a training curriculum.
    (C) Publishing survey results.
    (D) Developing a national database.

91. According to the speaker, what will Mr. Letovsky do next?
    (A) Give a demonstration.
    (B) Tour a facility.
    (C) Talk to reporters.
    (D) Receive an award.

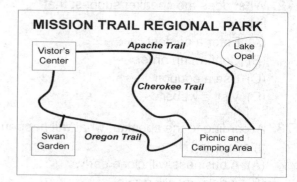

92. Who most likely are the listeners?
    (A) Maintenance workers.
    (B) Bus drivers.
    (C) Tourists.
    (D) Park rangers.

93. Look at the graphic. Where will the listeners be unable to go today?
    (A) Lake Opal.
    (B) Swan Garden.
    (C) The Picnic and Camping Area.
    (D) The Visitor's Center.

94. What does the woman encourage the listeners to do?
    (A) Bring a map.
    (B) Check the weather forecast.
    (C) Store their belongings.
    (D) Use sun protection.

Booking Details:
CONFIRMED
Booking Date:
May 13

Booking Reference Number:
BVT90L9

Guest Details
Lambert, Todd

(00) 0 0123456 000000001 8

Route	Flight #
Chicago - Buenos Aires	SS870
Buenos Aires - Chicago	SS871

Departure	Arrival
June 12, 22:00	June 13, 12:00
June 24, 15:00	June 25, 05:00

95. What type of business does the speaker work for?
(A) A bookstore.
(B) A mobile phone carrier.
(C) An electronics store.
(D) A travel agency.

96. What does the speaker advise the listener to purchase?
(A) A different SIM card.
(B) A new computer.
(C) An insurance policy.
(D) An economy plane ticket.

97. Look at the graphic. What did the speaker send Mr. Lambert?
(A) A list of recommendations.
(B) A guidebook.
(C) A flight schedule.
(D) A pricing brochure.

CATERING ORDER FORM

Qty.	Item	Price
2	Fruit trays	2@15.00=30.00
3	Deli platters	2@25.00=50.00
24	Assorted pastries	24@1.50=36.00
20	Bottled water (16 oz.)	20@1.00=20.00
20	Soft drinks (12 oz. can)	20@0.75=15.00
		Total: 151.00

98. What type of event is being catered?
(A) A product launch.
(B) A business meeting.
(C) An academic lecture.
(D) A retirement party.

99. Look at the graphic. Which quantity on the original order form is no longer accurate?
(A) 2.
(B) 3.
(C) 20.
(D) 24.

100. What is the listener asked to do tomorrow?
(A) Arrive early to set up a room.
(B) Bring additional staff.
(C) Pick up an identification badge.
(D) Give a speech.

This is the end of the Listening test. Turn to Part 5 in your test book.

GO ON TO THE NEXT PAGE.

READING TEST

In the Reading test, you will read a variety of texts and answer several different types of reading comprehension questions. The entire Reading test will last 75 minutes. There are three parts, and directions are given for each part. You are encouraged to answer as many questions as possible within the time allowed.

You must mark your answers on the separate answer sheet. Do not write your answers in your test book.

PART 5

Directions: A word or phrase is missing in each of the sentences below. Four answer choices are given below each sentence. Select the best answer to complete the sentence. Then mark the letter (A), (B), (C), or (D) on your answer sheet.

101. Smoking is prohibited in this building, but employees ------- use the outdoor terrace if they wish to smoke on their breaks.
(A) must
(B) may
(C) need to
(D) shall

102. Honoring retiring executives with a lavish party is a well-------- practice in this company.
(A) found
(B) intended
(C) known
(D) established

103. We are not sure when the work will be completed, but the supervisor gave us a(n) ------- of three weeks.
(A) estimate
(B) approximate
(C) decision
(D) deduction

104. The Morenos were disappointed to find out that there were no more tickets ------- for the concert.
(A) vacant
(B) present
(C) available
(D) inclusive

105. Most employees, ------- those with spouses and children, are worried about the proposed changes to the company health plan.
(A) especially
(B) surprisingly
(C) such as
(D) in turn

106. All of the recent sales figures ------- that the new advertising campaign has been successful.
(A) specify
(B) announce
(C) indicate
(D) classify

107. As soon as the hairdresser was finished, Mrs. Jones looked at ------- apprehensively in the mirror.
(A) hers
(B) himself
(C) that
(D) herself

108. The contract is so vaguely worded that several items are open to -------.
(A) interpretation
(B) suspicion
(C) commission
(D) invention

14

109. Janice is not very good at networking in her field because she is reluctant to ------- people she does not know.
(A) appear
(B) approach
(C) approve
(D) applaud

110. ------- upon finishing the urgent report, Dale printed it and took it directly to the vice president.
(A) As soon as
(B) Immediately
(C) Once
(D) No sooner than

111. The police officer claimed that he did not have the ------- to intervene in the argument between the two men.
(A) purpose
(B) altitude
(C) authority
(D) proposal

112. Stephanie has emailed the client and left several telephone messages, but there has been no ------- from him so far.
(A) respond
(B) responded
(C) response
(D) responsible

113. I don't understand how Jim could have confused the two packages because they are not at all -------.
(A) ideal
(B) similar
(C) relative
(D) familiar

114. For the past ten years, the financial services ------- of the economy has been growing the most rapidly.
(A) zone
(B) sector
(C) extent
(D) district

115. We would rather pay more to have the machine fixed properly than risk a ------- of the problem.
(A) reverberation
(B) restoration
(C) reoccurrence
(D) revision

116. The legal department has promised that the new contracts will be ------- by this Wednesday.
(A) finalized
(B) finishing
(C) finally
(D) finite

117. The doctor explained that the surgery included several difficult -------, but that the overall success rate was still good.
(A) symptoms
(B) actions
(C) conclusions
(D) procedures

118. For single parents, one of the great ------- of working at this company is the flexible working hours.
(A) welfares
(B) interests
(C) benefits
(D) aptitudes

119. The computer can handle these mathematical ------- much more quickly than any human can.
(A) formulas
(B) solutions
(C) prescriptions
(D) explanations

120. Unfortunately, it is not our ------- to accept returns of merchandise unless the customer has proof of purchase.
(A) strategy
(B) primacy
(C) policy
(D) progeny

GO ON TO THE NEXT PAGE.

121. There was an ------- when the company spokesperson announced that all employees would have to accept a pay cut.
(A) upswell
(B) uncertain
(C) unbalance
(D) uproar

122. Although there is not much demand for the toys in this country, we are able to ------- a significant amount to countries in Europe.
(A) export
(B) extract
(C) explain
(D) except

123. ------- Tina is a medical doctor, her twin sister is an accomplished ballerina.
(A) Because
(B) However
(C) Since
(D) While

124. Laboratory tests of the new medicine have been very -------, so the company plans to go ahead with its development.
(A) dubious
(B) suspicious
(C) promising
(D) talented

125. The relationship between management and ------- has been difficult in the past, but these days most employees are happy with their working conditions.
(A) service
(B) employment
(C) work
(D) labor

126. The witness was unable to ------- the suspect because he had changed his appearance since committing the crime.
(A) clarify
(B) identify
(C) ratify
(D) classify

127. Only twelve ------- of those who responded to the survey rated our customer service as being well above average.
(A) percent
(B) percents
(C) portions
(D) percentage

128. Greg had been employed as an accountant ever ------- his graduation from university.
(A) after
(B) X
(C) though
(D) since

129. One of the ------- problems with this plan is the lack of support among certain departments in the company.
(A) most
(C) mutual
(B) merely
(D) major

130. Legislators predict that it will be very difficult to find enough support for the ------- new law.
(A) decisive
(B) commercial
(C) widespread
(D) controversial

Directions: Read the texts that follow. A word or phrase is missing in some of the sentences. Four answer choices are given below each of the sentences. Select the best answer to complete the text. Then mark the letter (A), (B), (C), or (D) on your answer sheet.

Questions 131-134 refer to the following e-mail.

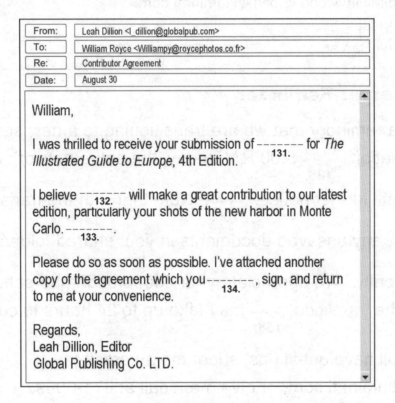

From:	Leah Dillion <l_dillion@globalpub.com>
To:	William Royce <Williampy@roycephotos.co.fr>
Re:	Contributor Agreement
Date:	August 30

William,

I was thrilled to receive your submission of --------- for *The Illustrated Guide to Europe*, 4th Edition.
                                          131.

I believe --------- will make a great contribution to our latest
          132.
edition, particularly your shots of the new harbor in Monte Carlo. ---------.
                      133.

Please do so as soon as possible. I've attached another copy of the agreement which you---------, sign, and return
                                          134.
to me at your convenience.

Regards,
Leah Dillion, Editor
Global Publishing Co. LTD.

131. (A) tickets
(B) contracts
(C) comments
(D) photographs

132. (A) your
(B) they
(C) his
(D) them

133. (A) However, I noticed that you have not signed the contributor agreement
(B) Unless you have another idea, we should stick to the schedule as posted
(C) To get started, select an option in the list and click on the link
(D) This email was sent from a notification-only address that cannot accept incoming email

134. (A) must have downloaded
(B) had downloaded
(C) can download
(D) must be downloading

GO ON TO THE NEXT PAGE

Illuminati Industries

Memo

To: All staff members <all.recipients@illuminati.com>
From: Colin Haywood <colin@illuminati.com>
Date: August 4
Re: New Server

New Server Reminder

This is a reminder that we are transitioning to a new server

configuration. ------- 5:00 P.M. today, the entire network will be
                   135.

down until further notice. --------. Note that with the transition
                            136.

process, any unsaved documents in your shared folders -------
                                                    137.

permanently. We appreciate your cooperation and patience

during the transition, ------- may take up to 24 hours to complete.
                      138.

If you still have questions, shoot me an email at:

colin@illuminati.com, or give me a call at 871-0099.

---

135. (A) Due to
(B) As of
(C) Prior to
(D) Aside from

136. (A) Again, it is essential that all employees refrain
from using the restroom during the renovation
process
(B) Hence, workers will remove any items left in the
stairways, hallways, and common areas
(C) Therefore, please remember to return your
security badges at the end of the work week
(D) Thus, it is important that you have save back-up
copies of any files which you may need

137. (A) have to delete
(B) were deleted
(C) to delete
(D) will be deleted

138. (A) which
(B) in addition
(C) so that
(D) then

From:	Ben Chen <bchen@justducky.com>
To:	Kim Hastings <hastyk@hardhat.com>
Re:	Just Ducky Web Site
Date:	August 14

✉ Product catalog 2.3 MB

Hey Kim,

Just Ducky will receive its fall product line shortly. _____ we need to update
                                                        139.
the Just Ducky Web site to reflect these changes and promote our new items.
I'd like the home page to feature the County Cork ceramic pottery line, which is
exceedingly hard to find. We are one of only two retailers in the country allowed
to offer County Cork products, so we really want it _____ on the site.
                                                    140.

Meanwhile, I would like to update the online shopping page to reflect a wide
variety of changes, i.e. merchandise that is out of stock, or we no longer carry.

_____. Please select the most attractive _____ to use on the site.
141.   **142.**

Thank you,
Ben Chen
General manager, Just Ducky

139. (A) Nevertheless
(B) Likewise
(C) Moreover
(D) Accordingly

140. (A) emphasizing
(B) emphasized
(C) emphasizes
(D) emphasize

141. (A) I have attached our new catalog, which also
contains photos of relevant products
(B) I have scheduled a luncheon and attached a
list of potential guests
(C) I will visit the facility next week and attach my
findings
(D) I will meet with Mr. Robbins, who also happens
to be fond of hard-to-find pottery

142. (A) images
(B) explanations
(C) charts
(D) catalogs

GO ON TO THE NEXT PAGE.

INTEROFFICE MEMORANDUM

TO: ALL IVERSON DESIGN ASSOCIATES
FROM: LEONARD RUBIN, DIR. OF RECRUITMENT
SUBJECT: MARKETING AAE
DATE: 11/3
CC: NONE

IMMEDIATE OPENING

Iverson Design has an immediate opening for an assistant account executive in our marketing department.

Strong computer skills and a working knowledge of content branding are -------. Candidates with experience in sales and a minimum of
143.
three years in online marketing are preferred. At this time we are accepting applications from ------- candidates only. -------.
144.   **145.**

A more detailed ------- of the position can be found at
146.
www.frankdesco.com/joinus.

143. (A) necessitate
     (B) necessary
     (C) necessitating
     (D) necessarily

144. (A) internal
     (B) international
     (C) recent
     (D) early

145. (A) We design and implement solutions for our customers
     (B) As part of the trial period, each workday, the writer will be provided a list of articles from different websites
     (C) However, if we don't receive a sufficient number of applications from qualified Iverson associates, the position will be opened to the public
     (D) Please leave your name and telephone number, and one of our technicians will return your call shortly

146. (A) narrative
     (B) description
     (C) commentary
     (D) critique

PART 7

Directions: In this part you will read a selection of texts, such as magazine and newspaper articles, e-mails, and instant messages. Each text or set of texts is followed by several questions. Select the best answer for each question and mark the letter (A), (B), (C), or (D) on your answer sheet.

Questions 147-148 refer to the following Web site.

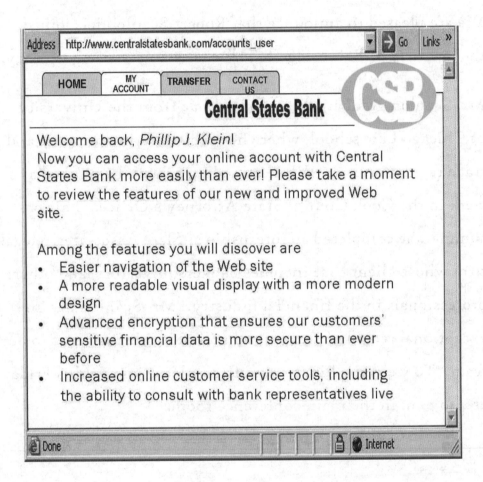

147. Who most likely is Mr. Klein?
   (A) A bank customer.
   (B) A bank executive.
   (C) A bank consultant.
   (D) A designer of the bank Web site.

148. What is NOT mentioned as a feature of the new Web site?
   (A) Greater security of information.
   (B) The addition of customer service options.
   (C) Enhanced visual design.
   (D) A listing of all service fees.

GO ON TO THE NEXT PAGE.

Bainbridge & Havens

Attorneys at Law

Since 1971

We are pleased to announce that Robert Scanlon has joined the law firm of Bainbridge & Havens as an associate attorney.

Mr. Scanlon graduated *magna cum laude* from the University of Chicago Law school, where he specialized in anti-trust and trade regulation law. While attending school, he worked as a clerk in the Cook County State Attorney's Office. This past summer, he completed an internship at Slate Associates, a legal firm whose client base includes bankers, investors, and other professionals in the financial industry. Mr. Scanlon has an exceptional record of service and will be a valuable asset to our team. To welcome him to our office, please join us this Friday at 4:30 p.m. in the main conference room.

149. Where is the notice most likely posted?
(A) In a bank.
(B) In an investment firm.
(C) In a law office.
(D) In a government agency.

150. What are employees invited to do on Friday?
(A) Attend a professional conference.
(B) Meet a new staff member.
(C) Watch a musical performance.
(D) Join a community service group.

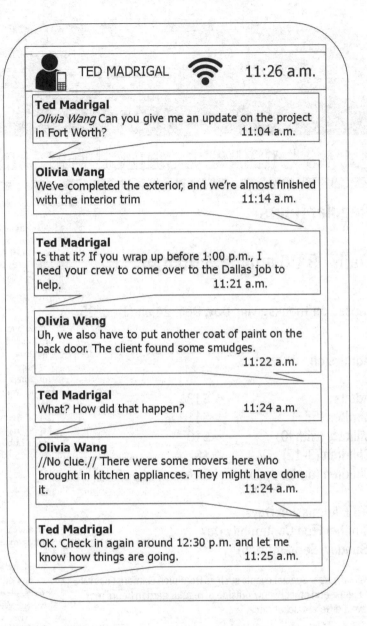

151. What type of business does Mr. Madrigal work for?

(A) A painting service.

(B) A real estate firm.

(C) A furniture store.

(D) A moving company.

152. At 11:24 a.m. what does Ms. Wang most likely mean when she writes "No clue"?

(A) She cannot guess how long a task will take.

(B) She does not know for sure how the problem was caused.

(C) She has identified the cause of a problem.

(D) She is asking for additional materials.

GO ON TO THE NEXT PAGE.

Lewis Gunther Botanical Gardens

Regular Hours

Daily - 9:00 a.m. to 5:00 p.m.

Closed on Thanksgiving Day, Dec. 24 and Dec. 25

Admission

Adults	$13
Seniors (55+)	$11
Military (with ID)	$10
Children (3-12)	$8
Children (under 3)	Free

FREE Admission Days:
Gunther Free Community Day
(Sunday, September 5)

Please note – Special events such as Dominion Garden, Festival of Lights, and other events outside of regular garden hours may have a different ticket price.

Recognized as one of the top gardens in the U.S.; recently voted #3 in USA Now's Ten Best Gardens Contest

Private tours are available on Saturday and Sunday mornings, and can be arranged by contacting our events coordinator, Regis Lubb at (303)778-0022

For directions, for information on our exhibitions, and to view our events, please visit our Web site
www.guntherbotanical.com

---

153. What is indicated about Lewis Gunther Botanical Gardens?
- (A) It has an art gallery on-site.
- (B) Special events may have a different entry fee.
- (C) It features a playground for children.
- (D) It offers Monday hours upon request.

154. According to the information, how can private tours be arranged?
- (A) By submitting an online form.
- (B) By visiting the information desk.
- (C) By telephoning a staff member.
- (D) By paying a different admission price.

Burton Academy of Cinema

Stark Titan Studios Mini Film Festival Sat. June 20 8:00 p.m

The Burton Academy of Cinema is hosting a mini-festival of films produced by Hollywood's famed Stark Titan Studios. The first film of the series, Bonneville Nights, will be shown this Saturday, June 20, at 8:00 p.m. in the academy's Vista Theater, located inside Goodman Hall. Professor D.P. Steinhauser, author of Hollywood: Yesterday and Today, will introduce the first film made by Stark Titan Studios and give a brief lecture. The 1939 film was directed by Carl Noonan and stars renowned dramatic actress Jayne Graves.

Tickets can be purchased at the Vista Theater box office from 9:00 a.m. to 9:00 p.m. Admission to this event is $12 for students with BAC identification, and $18 for the general public. Passes for the mini-festival are available at the box office at a cost of $50 for students and $75 for the general public.

For a complete listing of mini-festival films and events, visit the academy's Web site: www.burtonac.org/mini_festival

Vista Theater Box Office: 602-922-1100

Arts Brevis Inc.

155. What is the notice mainly about?
(A) A professor's first publication.
(B) A class about acting.
(C) A film showing.
(D) A new theater.

156. What is indicated about D.P. Steinhauser?
(A) He attended BAC.
(B) He wrote a book about Hollywood cinema.
(C) He is featured in an old movie.
(D) He is Jayne Graves' husband.

157. What is mentioned about students at the academy?
(A) They are entitled to discounted admission.
(B) They can apply for employment at the theater box office.
(C) They should register for classes no later than June 20.
(D) They are required to take a course on the history of film.

GO ON TO THE NEXT PAGE.

CYCLE SPECTRUM

Arizona's Arizona's Premier Cyclery
Sales – Rentals – Service

Cycle Spectrum is pleased to announce the Grand Opening of its fifth shop in the East Valley this **Sunday, April 15**

We invite customers old and new to visit our newest location at Indian School Road and 40th Street in Old Scottsdale

COUPONS

All offers expire on May 15.
Coupons are single-use only and cannot be combined.

30% Off

Get 30% off any clothing purchase of $150 or more

Buy one bike at full price and get a complimentary helmet, odometer, or pair of gloves

Rent a bike for two days and get the third day at no additional cost

Store hours: 10:00 a.m. to 9:00 p.m. daily   **Tel: 707-440-1212**

158. What is being advertised?
(A) New bicycle models.
(B) A change in ownership.
(C) A new store location.
(D) An anniversary celebration.

159. According to the advertisement, how can customers receive a free cycling accessory?
(A) By purchasing a bicycle.
(B) By spending $150 on clothing.
(C) By visiting the store on a certain day.
(D) By renting a bicycle for a weekend.

160. What is indicated about the coupons?
(A) They will be distributed on April 15.
(B) They can be used by new customers only.
(C) They are accepted at all store locations.
(D) They can be used until May 15.

New Housing for Southern University

August 2 – A ground-breaking ceremony took place last Friday at the intersection of Jenkins Road and Sheffield Street in Lawrence, where Southern University is building a new mixed-use residential complex, Watterson Towers. University president Buck Levitt turned over the first shovelful of dirt in the site, located 100 yards north of the main campus. ---[1]---.

Watterson Towers is a joint venture between the university (a public institution) and Allied Partners (a local property development firm.) It will consist of twin 25-story buildings. ---[2]---. Allied will develop the site and manage the retail operations.

"Until recently, most of our students have been commuters." Mr. Levitt said "Now we're seeing a sharp increase in the number of applicants who request on-campus housing --- [3]---. The high-rise dormitory we built last spring has helped to some extent. But when this project is completed, we'll be in a much better position to serve our students." The complex and the campus will be connected by a scenic footpath.

Several retailers have already expressed interest in leasing space in the complex including a number of clothing stores and restaurants. ---[4]---. Dan Turner, Allied's chief architect, said that he is in talks with a supermarket chain interested in opening a new location.

- Trevor Timothy, Staff Reporter

161. Who is Mr. Levitt?
(A) A college administrator.
(B) A store clerk.
(C) An architect.
(D) A property developer.

162. What business is Dan Turner trying to attract to Watterson Towers?
(A) A movie theater.
(B) A bookstore.
(C) A supermarket.
(D) A fitness club.

163. In which of the positions marked [1], [2], [3], and [4] does the following sentence best belong?
"Each will have retail space at the ground level and student apartments on the upper floors."
(A) [1].
(B) [2].
(C) [3].
(D) [4].

GO ON TO THE NEXT PAGE.

Northwest Tradetalk

Volume 4
Issue 12

Published by The Northwest Trade Commission

Thatcher Group Sees Bright Future

Spokane International Airport (GEG) and the Thatcher Group are celebrating the opening of Aeroflow 365, the latest addition to GEG's ground support facilities. The facility, the largest of its kind at GEG, has a staff of 200, including 40 mechanics; additionally, it has an equipment repair shop, storage areas for spare parts, a washing and drying station, and a painting station. Aeroflow 365 was financed by the Thatcher Group, and is currently owned and managed by the group. Built and equipped at a cost of 34.9 million dollars, the facility services the ground support equipment of Thatcher Air, Northwest Airlines, and Alaskan Express. The group decided the time was right to expand the maintenance services available at the airport.

"All mechanical equipment is subject to wear and tear," stated Kevin Shipp, head of Operations and Logistical Support at Aeroflow 365. "With such rapid addition of flights, the systems were becoming strained. Our goal was to get ahead of potential malfunctions by building in more maintenance capacity before minor inconveniences became genuine problems."

Shipp added that passengers are most likely to notice the effects of Aeroflow 365 first-hand when checking in and claiming their baggage. "With properly running conveyor belts, check-in is likely to be a lot smoother. Moreover, because more baggage carts will be operational, luggage will arrive more quickly in the baggage claim areas. And, of course, fewer flights will be delayed as loading and unloading cargo and supplies will take the ground crew less time."

164. According to the article, why was Aeroflow 365 built?

(A) There were increasing demands on the maintenance services.

(B) The airport's three newest airlines wanted to have their own facility.

(C) There was no similar facility available at the airport.

(D) Existing facilities needed to be closed for renovation.

165. What is indicated about the Thatcher Group?

(A) It owns Spokane International Airport.

(B) It has offices in multiple countries.

(C) It plans to hire 365 additional employees.

(D) It has invested $34.9 million in ground support improvements.

166. What do some workers the at Aeroflow 365 facility do?

(A) Maintain airport runways.

(B) Construct new airplanes.

(C) Load and unload baggage.

(D) Assist passengers with ticketing.

167. What is NOT listed as a benefit that Aeroflow 365 will offer passengers?

(A) Passengers will be able to check in with greater ease.

(B) Passengers will experience fewer flight delays.

(C) Passengers will be able to collect their luggage more quickly.

(D) Passengers will enjoy lower ticket prices.

GO ON TO THE NEXT PAGE.

Protecting your personal financial future

We at the D.W. Foreman Group are committed to helping our clients achieve their financial goals. Our team of consultants will help you design a personal investment plan aimed at ensuring your financial security over the long term. Founded in San Diego more than four decades ago as Donald Whistler Foreman Accounting, the D.W. Foreman Group has grown from a relatively obscure firm to one of the most respected institutions of its kind.

We pride ourselves in:

Accessibility - Unlike many of our competitors, we make sure our consultants focus on a limited number of accounts. When our client base expands, we simply hire more consultants. So whenever you have a question, need, or concern, you can speak to someone the same day that you call.

Innovation - Our cutting-edge software enables us to produce a wide array of financial reports and projections to give you the information you need, often at a moment's notice.

Foreman Group Senior Staff:

Philadelphia
Irving Chapman, Global Specialist
ichapman@dwforemangroup.com

San Diego
Sofia Krespi, President
skrespi@dwforemangroup.com

New York
Brandon Sweeney, Loan Specialist
bsweeney@dwforemangroup.com

Lutetia Brown, Real Estate Specialist
lbrown@dwforemangroup.com

Seattle
Abe Stone, Domestic Specialist
astone@dwforemangroup.com

Experience - We employ only the most experienced and knowledgeable consultants, all of whom have advanced degrees in economics or finance from leading universities. Our staff also includes specialists in international markets who are eager to share their insights into foreign investing.

For more information, please visit our Web site at www.dwforemangroup.com

168. What type of service does the D.W. Foreman Group provide?
(A) Computer support.
(B) Business marketing.
(C) Financial planning.
(D) Building construction.

169. What is indicated about D.W. Foreman Group?
(A) It was established by Sofia Krespi.
(B) It used to have a different name.
(C) It offers lower prices than its competitors.
(D) It has recently merged with another company.

170. What is suggested about the D.W. Foreman Group consultants?
(A) They travel extensively.
(B) They teach at local universities.
(C) They use advanced computer programs.
(D) They manage as many clients as they want.

171. What is mentioned about Mr. Chapman?
(A) He is an expert in international investment.
(B) He works in Seattle.
(C) He is a newly hired consultant.
(D) He works in the same office as Ms. Brown.

GO ON TO THE NEXT PAGE

From:	Veronica Goss
To:	All Staff
Re:	Centix Technologies
Date:	December 2

Fellow employees,

In an effort to reduce our company's energy consumption, the Environmental Advisory Board has decided to purchase a new automation system from Centix Technologies. The office-wide system will automatically regulate thermostats and overhead lighting to accommodate our usual work schedules.

For example, at 8:00 p.m. each weekday, all office lights will automatically be turned off or dimmed (except for hallway and stairwell lights). Likewise, on Saturdays and Sundays, the temperature will be maintained at a steady 70°F instead of the 72°F during the week. This new system should help reduce our monthly utility bills by up to 15% and help us meet our conservational goals.

We acknowledge that some of you will be affected by these changes more than others, particularly those whose schedules do not conform to regular working hours. If this situation applies to you, feel free to contact the personnel department to request an office change, as some sections of the building will be set to a later schedule. Bring any other concern to your supervisor.

Sincerely,
Veronica Goss, Vice President of Operations

172. What is the purpose of the e-mail?
(A) To encourage employees to develop more efficient work habits.
(B) To offer employees the opportunity to work from home.
(C) To clarify the requirements of a new environmental law.
(D) To explain an upcoming change in workplace conditions.

173. The word "maintained" in paragraph 2, line 3, is closet in meaning
(A) taken.
(B) kept.
(C) confirmed.
(D) repaired.

174. What is mentioned as a benefit of the Centix product?
(A) It can be serviced from outside the office.
(B) It can be used in any work environment.
(C) It will save the company money.
(D) It will reduce employee workloads.

175. What are employees who advised to do?
(A) Change their work schedules.
(B) Take work home over the weekend.
(C) Talk to Ms. Goss.
(D) Consider switching offices.

From:	<customercare@ballatinecharlotte.com>
To:	<tan_nguyen@aimconsulting.com>
Re:	Reservation CBS101087
Date:	October 22

Dear Mr. Nguyen,

Thank you for choosing Ballantine Suites Charlotte. Per your request, nine rooms have been reserved for your group.

Because you will be participating in the National Consulting Symposium to be held here at the hotel in early November, your group is receiving a special rate of $149 per night, per room.

Our records show an arrival date of November 3 and a departure date of November 9 for all members of your group. The reservation is held under your name. Please note the reservation number CBS101087, which you need to reference for any communication with us regarding your stay.

We know your group will enjoy our luxurious hotel. In addition to our beautiful and relaxing atrium, outdoor pool, and state-of-the-art facilities, we also offer a variety of dining options. The Dunhill Tavern, located near the lobby, offers casual fare.

If you are interested in five-star dining, try our Trattoria D'Oro. Reservations are highly recommended but not required.

We look forward to seeing you in November.

Thank you for choosing Ballantine Suites Charlotte.

The Customer Care Team at Ballantine Suites Charlotte

GO ON TO THE NEXT PAGE.

From:	<tan_nguyen@aimconsulting.com>
To:	<customercare@ballatinecharlotte.com>
Re:	Reservation CBS101087
Date:	October 23

To whom it may concern,

My confirmation number is CBS101087, and I am writing to clarify some errors in my booking confirmation. I requested ten rooms, not nine. In addition, although the rest of my group will be checking in on the eve of the conference, I will not be arriving until November 4.

The above information was indicated on my original request. Please make applicable changes to the reservation and notify me when the corrections have been completed.

Thank you for your prompt attention to this matter.

Tan Nguyen

176. What information in the hotel records is incorrect?
(A) Dates of the conference.
(B) Number of rooms.
(C) Payment method.
(D) Check-out times.

177. What is the purpose of the first e-mail?
(A) To answer a question about a hotel's amenities.
(B) To arrange for transportation.
(C) To explain a change in hotel rates.
(D) To confirm the details of a reservation.

178. What is suggested about Trattoria D'Oro?
(A) It recently opened.
(B) It is often busy.
(C) It is next to the Ballantine Ballroom.
(D) It has been renovated.

179. What is stated about Mr. Nguyen?
(A) He will arrive later than the rest of his group.
(B) He will not be attending the conference.
(C) He does not want to share a room with his colleague.
(D) He was misinformed about room rates.

180. In the second e-mail, the word "matter" in paragraph 3, is closest in meaning to
(A) substance.
(B) choice.
(C) length.
(D) situation.

Join the Branford Ramblers!

On June 7, the Branford Recreation Committee approved the creation of the Branford Ramblers Hiking Club at Branford Memorial Park.

The hiking club will meet from Monday through Friday at noon, and the activity will run throughout the summer. The club will meet at the trailhead by the park's entrance at Page Boulevard.

Each participant should wear comfortable hiking shoes and bring a bottle of drinking water.

Interested residents should call or visit the park's Recreation Office to register.

The club will officially meet after a minimum of five members have joined. Please check the calendar for any updates or changes. For more information, contact club coordinator Tripp Philbin at 303-544-0100.

GO ON TO THE NEXT PAGE.

Steven D. Branford Memorial Park
Weekly Activities Calendar for the Month of July

Mondays	Tuesdays	Wednesdays	Thursdays	Fridays	Saturdays
12:00 p.m. Branford Ramblers Hiking Club (South Trail)	12:00 p.m. Branford Ramblers Hiking Club (South Trail)	12:00 p.m. Branford Ramblers Hiking Club (South Trail)	12:00 p.m. Branford Ramblers Hiking Club (South Trail)	9:30 a.m. Community Clean-Up (Jetson Harbor)	10:00 a.m. "The Art of Nature" Painting for Children (Dobson Art Center) $10 fee, includes lunch
5:30 p.m. Community Badminton (Grover Courts)	12:15 p.m. "Lunch and Learn" Bird-watching (Victor Pavilion) $5 fee, includes lunch	5:30 p.m. Community Badminton (Grover Courts)	12:15 p.m. "Lunch and Learn" Local flora (Victor Pavilion) $5 fee, includes lunch	12:00 p.m. Branford Ramblers Hiking Club (South Trail)	2:00 p.m. Branford Historical Tour (Rancher House) $25 includes full-color commemorative guidebook
			5:30 p.m. Pick-up Basketball League (2nd & 4th weeks) (Recreation Arena)	5:30 P.M. Community Badminton (West Court)	

For more detailed information about any of the events listed above, please contact the park's Recreation Office at 513-909-1233.

181. What is the purpose of the notice?
    (A) To announce a new activity at a park.
    (B) To share the agenda for a board meeting.
    (C) To request volunteers to lead a club.
    (D) To present a proposal for a new trail at a park.

182. In the notice, the word "run" in line 5, is closest in meaning to
    (A) reach.
    (B) grow.
    (C) jog.
    (D) continue.

183. What activity occurs only twice in July?
    (A) Community Badminton.
    (B) "Lunch and Learn".
    (C) Pick-up basketball.
    (D) Painting.

184. What is suggested about the hiking club in July?
    (A) It meets less frequently than originally planned.
    (B) Its coordinator is being replaced.
    (C) It provides bottled water to participants.
    (D) It meets at the same location each day.

185. What is indicated about Branford Memorial Park?
    (A) It is overseen by Tripp Philbin.
    (B) It has programs specifically for children.
    (C) Its Recreation Office is on Page Boulevard.
    (D) It has a swimming pool.

GO ON TO THE NEXT PAGE.

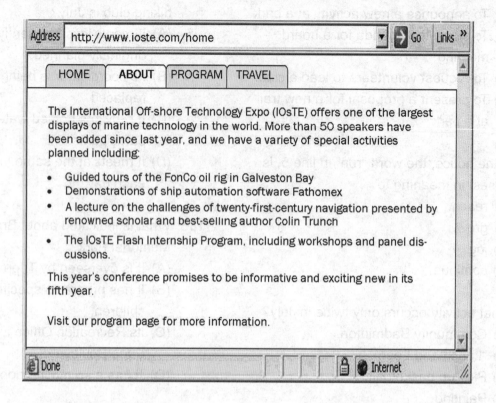

Address http://www.ioste.com/home   ▾ → Go   Links »

| HOME | **ABOUT** | PROGRAM | TRAVEL |

The International Off-shore Technology Expo (IOsTE) offers one of the largest displays of marine technology in the world. More than 50 speakers have been added since last year, and we have a variety of special activities planned including:

- Guided tours of the FonCo oil rig in Galveston Bay
- Demonstrations of ship automation software Fathomex
- A lecture on the challenges of twenty-first-century navigation presented by renowned scholar and best-selling author Colin Trunch
- The IOsTE Flash Internship Program, including workshops and panel discussions.

This year's conference promises to be informative and exciting new in its fifth year.

Visit our program page for more information.

Done   🔒 ● Internet

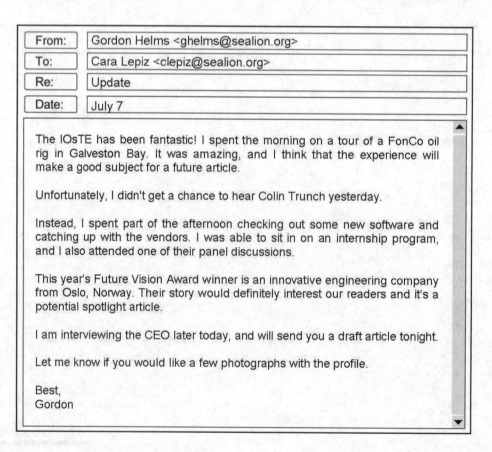

From:	Gordon Helms <ghelms@sealion.org>
To:	Cara Lepiz <clepiz@sealion.org>
Re:	Update
Date:	July 7

The IOsTE has been fantastic! I spent the morning on a tour of a FonCo oil rig in Galveston Bay. It was amazing, and I think that the experience will make a good subject for a future article.

Unfortunately, I didn't get a chance to hear Colin Trunch yesterday.

Instead, I spent part of the afternoon checking out some new software and catching up with the vendors. I was able to sit in on an internship program, and I also attended one of their panel discussions.

This year's Future Vision Award winner is an innovative engineering company from Oslo, Norway. Their story would definitely interest our readers and it's a potential spotlight article.

I am interviewing the CEO later today, and will send you a draft article tonight.

Let me know if you would like a few photographs with the profile.

Best,
Gordon

From:	Gordon Helms <ghelms@sealion.org>
To:	Oskar Strandell <strandell@maersk.com>
Re:	Photos
Date:	July 8

Dear Mr. Strandell,

It was great talking with you yesterday. I sent the article to my editor. She loved it and made an additional request. So I wonder if it's possible for us to meet briefly and take some photographs before you depart the Expo.

I'm confident that images would enhance the appeal of the story.

Respectfully,
Gordon Helms

186. According to Mr. Helms, what conference activity was he unable to attend?
(A) A guided tour.
(B) A panel discussion.
(C) A lecture.
(D) A workshop.

187. Who most likely is Mr. Helms?
(A) A travel agent.
(B) A journalist.
(C) An engineer.
(D) A magazine publisher.

188. In the first e-mail, the word "spotlight" paragraph 4, line 3 closest in meaning to
(A) featured.
(B) discarded.
(C) casual.
(D) bright.

189. What is indicated about IOsTE?
(A) It has increased the number of its presenters.
(B) It has increased the length of the event.
(C) It is designed for newcomers to the industry.
(D) It is held in a different country each year.

190. What is suggested about Mr. Strandell?
(A) He will be speaking at next year's conference.
(B) He met Mr. Helms.
(C) He is a well-known photographer.
(D) He was recently promoted.

GO ON TO THE NEXT PAGE.

R.B. Olds
19901 Clarendon Hills Road
Overland Park, KS 66214

Dear Mr. Olds,

Enclosed are three author copies of your new self-help book, *Concepts Unlimited*. It is now available for purchase on our Web site, www.oakparkpress.com, and it will be sold in select bookstores beginning May 3. So far, online sales of your book have been brisk, and we expect sales to increase.

In addition to your complimentary copies, you can buy more copies of your book at 50 percent off (use the online form on our Web site to order). This discount is also available for the other books you have authored, *Get Rich Now* and *Help Yourself to Success*.

As our valued author, you are also entitled to receive 15 percent off any other books published by Oak Park Press.

Thank you for choosing Oak Park Press.

Warm regards,
Oliver Grant

Author Order Form		
Author	R.B. OLDS	**OAK PARK PRESS**
Date	May 10	

# of Copies	Title	Price
5	Concepts Unlimited	25.00
4	Get Rich Now	20.00
2	Help Yourself to Success	10.00
	Sub-total	55.00

To purchase other books, please enter the author's name, the book title, and the desired number of copies in the corresponding boxes below:

# of Copies	Author	Title	Price
3	Rubin, M.	Maximum Wealth	27.00
		Total Amount Due	82.00

Note: Orders are shipped via standard mail and take two to three business days to arrive. If you choose the express option, we can deliver your order the very next day. Please contact customer support at (800)343-0909, Monday through Friday, 8:30 a.m. – 5:30 p.m. CST

Are you ready to proceed to your shopping cart?

YES☒

NO ☐

GO ON TO THE NEXT PAGE.➤

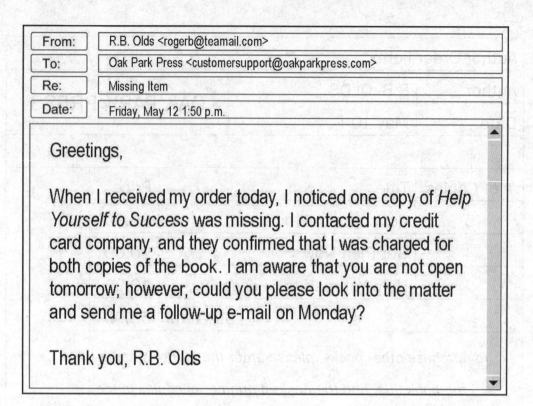

From:	R.B. Olds <rogerb@teamail.com>
To:	Oak Park Press <customersupport@oakparkpress.com>
Re:	Missing Item
Date:	Friday, May 12 1:50 p.m.

Greetings,

When I received my order today, I noticed one copy of *Help Yourself to Success* was missing. I contacted my credit card company, and they confirmed that I was charged for both copies of the book. I am aware that you are not open tomorrow; however, could you please look into the matter and send me a follow-up e-mail on Monday?

Thank you, R.B. Olds

191. In the letter, the word "brisk" in paragraph 1, line 4 is closest in meaning to
(A) fresh.
(B) strong.
(C) attentive.
(D) brief.

192. How many free copies of Concepts Unlimited have been sent to Mr. Olds?
(A) Two.
(B) Three.
(C) Four.
(D) Eight.

193. What is most likely true about Mr. Olds?
(A) One of his books is out of stock.
(B) He has switched to a new marketing agency.
(C) All of his books are bestsellers.
(D) He selected the express delivery option.

194. What is indicated about Maximum Wealth, Minimum Effort?
(A) It will be sold to Mr. Olds at a 15 percent discount.
(B) It was written collaboratively by Mr. Olds and Mr. Rubin.
(C) It received positive reviews from book critics.
(D) It will be available in select stores starting May 3.

195. What is suggested about customer support?
(A) It is managed by Mr. Grant.
(B) It does not deal with shipping issues.
(C) It is located in Overland Park.
(D) It does not operate on weekends.

From:	dee_lochirco@scoville-prentice.com
To:	walker@tcbdistribution.com
Re:	Presentation
Date:	December 17

Edward,

I've just landed in Albuquerque and I am writing now from the airport. Predictably, the airline lost my checked luggage, which will unfortunately affect our meeting arrangements tomorrow. Although my multimedia presentation is on the hard drive of my laptop, which was in my carry-on, the cosmetic product samples that you need to see are in the missing luggage. The airline says the suitcase should be delivered to my hotel no later than the day after tomorrow, so I'm in a tough spot. Is there any way we could postpone tomorrow's demonstration until later in the week? Please let me know

Sincerely,
Dee Lo Chirco

Property Recovery Report

Please accept our apologies for the inconvenience caused by the mishandling of your baggage. We will use the information you provide to track and recover your belongings as quickly as possible.

To expedite the process, please provide a description of each bag along with a detailed list of the contents.

Report #	PRR121716
Passenger	Dee LoChirco
Email address	dee_lochirco@scoville-prentiss.com
Home address	5400 W. Cherokee Road Boulder, CO 80303
Temporary address (if required)	Top Western Rio Grade Suites 1015 Rio Grande Blvd NW, Albuquerque, NM 87104

Flight Number	Date(s)	Departure City	Arrival City	Comments
7J311	December 16	Seattle	Denver	
7J313	December 17	Denver	Albuquerque	

Type of Bag	Color	Manufacturer/Model
Large roller suitcase	Black	Crosby

Quantity	Description	Value
1	Various cosmetics	$150.00
1	Tikon DL-90 digital camera	$500.00
1	Charging cable	$50.00
1	Rony Vista portable projector	$1,500.00
1	Bluetooth wireless speaker	$200.00
1	Travel guide	$15.00
1	Various clothing (Pants, shirts, shoes, etc.)	$800.00

GO ON TO THE NEXT PAGE.

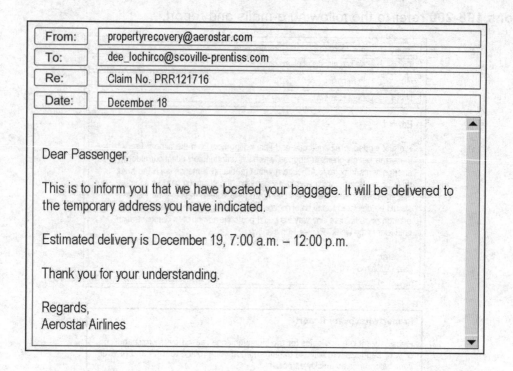

From:	propertyrecovery@aerostar.com
To:	dee_lochirco@scoville-prentiss.com
Re:	Claim No. PRR121716
Date:	December 18

Dear Passenger,

This is to inform you that we have located your baggage. It will be delivered to the temporary address you have indicated.

Estimated delivery is December 19, 7:00 a.m. – 12:00 p.m.

Thank you for your understanding.

Regards,
Aerostar Airlines

196. What does Ms. LoChirco indicate about the multimedia presentation?
(A) It will be sent by e-mail.
(B) It needs to be shortened.
(C) It has been lost.
(D) It is ready to go.

197. What does Ms. LoChirco ask Edward to do?
(A) Reschedule a meeting.
(B) Pick her up from the airport.
(C) Drive her to the hotel.
(D) Prepare product samples.

198. What does Ms. LoChirco want to present?
(A) Books.
(B) Clothes.
(C) Cosmetics.
(D) Electronics.

199. In the report the word "track" in paragraph 1, line 2, is closest in meaning to
(A) trace.
(B) copy.
(C) record.
(D) draw.

200. Where will the delivery be sent?
(A) To Seattle.
(B) To Albuquerque.
(C) To Boulder.
(D) To Denver.

Stop! This is the end of the test. If you finish before time is called, you may go back to Parts 5, 6, and 7 and check your work.

New TOEIC Listening Script

PART 1

1. (   ) (A) Two girls are dancing.
   (B) They are at the beach.
   (C) It is raining.
   (D) There is snow on the ground.

2. (   ) (A) They are boarding a train.
   (B) They are playing a game.
   (C) They are watching TV.
   (D) They are having lunch.

3. (   ) (A) They are on a rooftop.
   (B) They are on a boat.
   (C) They are in a library.
   (D) They are in a bank.

4. (   ) (A) He is surfing the Internet.
   (B) He is making copies.
   (C) He is reading a book.
   (D) He is sleeping at his desk.

5. (   ) (A) The girl is wearing a scarf.
   (B) The boy is wearing a jacket.
   (C) The man is wearing a hat.
   (D) The woman is wearing sunglasses.

6. (   ) (A) They are fighting.
   (B) They are walking.
   (C) They are eating.
   (D) They are kissing.

GO ON TO THE NEXT PAGE.

PART 2

7. (　　) Does the catering for the luncheon need to be picked up?
    (A) It was 15 dollars.
    (B) No, it's already been delivered.
    (C) The grocery store closes then.

8. (　　) Isn't my magazine subscription renewed automatically?
    (A) Yes, unless you cancel it.
    (B) The article on page 28.
    (C) She's a new subscriber.

9. (　　) When will Celine send out the meeting schedule?
    (A) Usually by e-mail.
    (B) Sometime this afternoon.
    (C) Only for part-time work.

10. (　　) Where did Eddie put the blueprints for the firm's new headquarters?
    (A) It'll be built on an empty lot in circle field.
    (B) He's showing it to the board of directors right now.
    (C) A well-known architecture firm.

11. (　　) Who should I show my safety training certificate to?
    (A) It's a twelve-hour course.
    (B) To your project manager.
    (C) Because the program is finished.

12. (　　) Can you help me distribute flyers downtown tomorrow?
    (A) How many do you need to hand out?
    (B) An office building on Riverdale Drive.
    (C) Yes, flight number 262.

13. (　　) Could you show me the sales figures from last week?
    (A) Some new merchandise.
    (B) Either way is fine.
    (C) I'll print you a copy.

14. (　　) Should we pack the copier parts in one box or in separate boxes?
    (A) We had to take separate flights.
    (B) Loading docks, six and seven.
    (C) They should go in multiple boxes.

15. (　　) Should I submit my travel expense form tomorrow?

    (A) It's not due until next week.

    (B) Let me know when you arrive.

    (C) Because the ticket was quite expensive.

16. (　　) Why are the letters of reference not attached to this resume?

    (A) Tomorrow afternoon.

    (B) Yes, at the conclusion of the interview.

    (C) They weren't provided by the applicant.

17. (　　) How often does the shuttle to the airport run?

    (A) No, I don't travel very often.

    (B) The fare is quite reasonable.

    (C) Every 15 minutes.

18. (　　) Do you work until 9 p.m. tonight?

    (A) Traffic was awful on the way in this morning.

    (B) I ate there recently.

    (C) Yes, many people are on vacation.

19. (　　) Who are we sending to the convention this year?

    (A) About a month from now.

    (B) Jenny and David.

    (C) A ticket to Pittsburgh.

20. (　　) Didn't Bill call in sick yesterday?

    (A) No, he was with some clients.

    (B) Yes, we're going outside.

    (C) I am feeling better, thanks.

21. (　　) You should open an account at Bank of East America.

    (A) I already have an account there.

    (B) It was on your desk last time I checked.

    (C) He's not a customer.

22. (　　) The post office is on this street, isn't it?

    (A) I believe so.

    (B) Sure, I'd be happy to.

    (C) An exhibit of Spanish pottery.

GO ON TO THE NEXT PAGE.

23. (　　) Are you going to next month's innovation seminar?
    (A) Chicago, I think.
    (B) Yes, I'm looking forward to it.
    (C) Social media.

24. (　　) Why don't you ask Ronald to give you a hand?
    (A) It was very helpful.
    (B) No, I forgot.
    (C) He's on a sales call right now.

25. (　　) Where would you like me to store these tables?
    (A) Enough for 20 people.
    (B) Stack them against the back wall, please.
    (C) By tomorrow morning at the latest.

26. (　　) What's the bestselling video camera at your store?
    (A) It's a high-quality recording.
    (B) This year, it's the JP-400.
    (C) Your camera will fit in this case.

27. (　　) How did you hear about the sale at Dan's Market?
    (A) There's an ad on the front page of the newspaper.
    (B) Sorry, she's on another line.
    (C) Yes, it's closed on Mondays.

28. (　　) When will Megan adjust our travel itinerary?
    (A) Only for full-time employees.
    (B) Usually by e-mail.
    (C) Hasn't she already done that?

29. (　　) Has either Tom or Irene applied for the assistant manager position?
    (A) It's a brand-new store.
    (B) Sure, I can use some help.
    (C) No, neither of them has.

30. (　　) How are we going to get from the airport to the conference center?
    (A) Twenty minutes from the airport.
    (B) Apparently, they had a nice trip.
    (C) A car will be there to drive us.

31. (   ) Would you call the technician who services the copier?
  (A) I already did.
  (B) He hasn't returned yet.
  (C) It's on your desk.

PART 3

Questions 32 through 34 *refer to the following conversation.*

M : Hi, my name is Randy Folkens and I'm calling because I bought tickets to see the Platinum Cheetah concert on Saturday night. I was told the tickets would arrive sometime last week, but I haven't received them yet.

W : Hmm, Folkens... Right. According to our records, I see that you ordered five tickets for this Saturday's performance. But for some reason they were never sent out. I apologize for this.

M : Well, it's a good thing I called then. I was worried that the tickets had been lost. Do you think I'll get them in time if you mail them out today?

W : Probably not. Since the concert is only a few days away, it's better if you pick up the tickets from the theater box office on the night of the performance.

32. (   ) Why is the man calling?
  (A) To confirm the date of a performance.
  (B) To buy some concert tickets.
  (C) To change the location of his seats.
  (D) To check the status of an order.

33. (   ) What problem does the woman mention?
  (A) An account was closed.
  (B) An event was postponed.
  (C) Some tickets were not sent out.
  (D) Some shipping addresses were wrong.

34. (   ) What does the woman suggest?
  (A) Checking a Web site.
  (B) Placing another order.
  (C) Using a different credit card.
  (D) Going to the box office.

Questions 35 through 37 *refer to the following phone conversation.*

W : Hi, this is Sharon Thomas from suite 502. I want to reserve the rooftop swimming pool for an event I'm planning. Is it available on Saturday, July 10?

GO ON TO THE NEXT PAGE.

M : Saturday, July 10... It's reserved from 12:00 to 3:00 p.m., but it's open after that.

W : OK, I guess that will work. From, say, 6:00 to 10:00 p.m.?

M : Yes, the pool area closes at 10:00.

W : Since it's going to be an evening event, I'd also like to use the barbecue grill. Is that possible?

M : Sure. However, there's an extra deposit. Fifty dollars, in addition to the $150 for the swimming pool. So that would be a $200 deposit. You'll get it back on Monday, provided you don't trash the facilities.

W : Oh, we won't. It will just be my family and a small group of adults celebrating my mother's birthday.

M : Great. I've got you penciled in for Saturday evening at the pool and reserved the grill. You'll have to come down to the administration office, fill out a reservation form, and pay the deposit before Friday at 5:00 p.m. The sooner, the better, actually.

35. (　　) What does the woman want to use?
    (A) A conference room.
    (B) A swimming pool.
    (C) Cleaning supplies.
    (D) Storage space.

36. (　　) What event is the woman planning?
    (A) A birthday celebration.
    (B) A wedding.
    (C) An anniversary.
    (D) A retirement party.

37. (　　) What does the woman have to do before Friday evening?
    (A) Pay a security deposit.
    (B) Return the equipment.
    (C) Return her keys.
    (D) Pick up her mother.

Questions 38 through 40 *refer to the following conversation.*

M : Excuse me, can you tell me what floor the shoe department is on?

W : Actually, our store sells shoes on two floors. Are you looking for anything in particular?

M : Yes, I'd like to buy a nice pair of dress shoes to wear for a wedding tonight. I flew here this morning and the airline lost the suitcase with my shoes in it.

W : I know how it is. Swift Airlines lost my luggage once, too. What a nightmare! But don't worry. You've come to the right place. We have a great selection of men's dress shoes. Take the elevator up to the fourth floor. There are plenty of sales reps on the floor to assist you.

38. (   ) Where most likely are the speakers?
        (A) At a department store.
        (B) At an airport.
        (C) At a bank.
        (D) At a restaurant.

39. (   ) What problem does the man mention?
        (A) He forgot his wallet.
        (B) He went to the wrong airport.
        (C) His flight was delayed.
        (D) His luggage was lost.

40. (   ) What does the woman tell the man to do?
        (A) Fill out a complaint form.
        (B) Come back later in the day.
        (C) Speak to a manager.
        (D) Go to the fourth floor.

Questions 41 through 43 refer to the following conversation.

W : I just got off the phone with Les Walker, the photographer from last year's annual company
    dinner. He said he'd be available again this year.

M : That's good news. He took great photographs last time and our company's grown so much
    since then. It'll be nice to get some photos of the new employees for our Web site.

W : Right, but we probably need to find a bigger place. Since we have more staff, I'm not sure
    we can all fit in the banquet hall we usually rent.

M : Do you have a head count yet? I'm sure you could call human resources and get an exact
    number of employees.

41. (   ) Who is Les Walker?
        (A) A hotel manager.
        (B) A photographer.
        (C) A Web site designer.
        (D) A lawyer.

42. (   ) According to the man, how has the company changed over the last year?
        (A) It has a new owner.
        (B) It has more employees.
        (C) It has expanded its product line.
        (D) It has merged with another firm.

GO ON TO THE NEXT PAGE

43. (   ) What is the woman concerned about?
      (A) The accuracy of a database.
      (B) The price of invitation.
      (C) The size of an event space.
      (D) The choices on a menu.

Questions 44 through 46 _refer to the following conversation between three speakers._

W : Hey guys, I'm going to see a play with a friend at the Cosmopolitan Theater this evening. Do you know if parking is easy to find around there?

Man A : Well, I went to a barber shop in that neighborhood last week. There's road construction near the theater, so there were fewer places to park than usual. Why don't you take the bus?

Man B : That's probably a better idea. Plus, I heard the theater's parking garage is partially under construction as well.

W : I guess I could just leave my car here in the lot overnight. Do you know which bus line stops at the theater?

Man A : Well, you can take the 54 Burton from Burnett Square all the way down to Market Street. It's a straight shot down Burton Avenue. Get off at Market and cross over to the south side of the street. From there, it's less than a two-minute walk to the theater.

Man B : Yeah, when you get off at Market, you'll see the kiosk for the theater on the left.

W : Um, I have a meeting later this afternoon, so what if I'll be coming from downtown?

Man B : Oh, in that case, you can take the subway straight to the theater; it's so much faster. Take the Red Line and get off at the Market/Hollywood stop. The exit is right in front of the theater.

44. (   ) What is the woman planning to do tonight?
      (A) Leave on vacation.
      (B) Meet with a client.
      (C) See a play.
      (D) Go out for dinner.

45. (   ) What does Man A recommend?
      (A) Arriving early.
      (B) Taking a bus.
      (C) Hiring a driver.
      (D) Reserving tickets.

46. (   ) What does Man B suggest?
      (A) Taking the subway.
      (B) Leaving later.
      (C) Going with a friend.
      (D) Asking for a refund.

Woman A : Darren, I heard you did a great job leading the meeting with Osborn Industries. They really liked the new marketing campaign we proposed. Especially the idea of advertising through social media.

M : Thanks, Leah. And I have a suggestion for future meetings. How about video conferencing instead of meeting face-to-face with our clients? It seems like a logical way for us to cut costs and lower our overhead. Especially since we're trying to expand our business globally.

Woman B : That's a good idea, Darren. But it seems like those video conferencing systems are consistently unreliable. Either the speakers' voices are garbled or the connection gets dropped altogether.

M : Well, Maggie, I just read an article about a new system that's been highly-rated. I'll send it to you when I'm back at my desk.

Woman A : Would you send me a copy of the article as well? I'm interested in at least looking into the idea.

M : Sure thing, Leah.

Woman B : Regardless of the potential for video conferencing, I don't think we should disregard the benefits of meeting with clients in person.

Woman A : //I hear you loud and clear, Leah.// And trust me, we're never going to do away with face-to-face client presentations. However, Ethan might be on to something.

47. ( ) Where do the speakers most likely work?
     (A) At a savings bank.
     (B) At a marketing agency.
     (C) At a technology firm.
     (D) At a television station.

48. ( ) What does Maggie say about video conferencing?
     (A) It tends to be problematic.
     (B) It will enable more employees to participate.
     (C) It allows for more frequent meetings.
     (D) It makes meetings easier to schedule.

49. ( ) What does Leah mean when she says, //"I hear you loud and clear, Leah."//?
     (A) She has a different point of view from Leah.
     (B) She doesn't understand what Leah said.
     (C) She agrees with Leah's statement.
     (D) She thinks Leah is speaking too loudly.

GO ON TO THE NEXT PAGE.

M : Cribb's Department Store. This is Darius speaking. How may I direct your call?

W : Hello, Darius. I'm not sure who I need to speak to about this. About eight months ago, I bought a sewing machine there. All of a sudden, it started making a terrible noise. Then smoke started coming out and it stopped working. So, I'd like to know if I can bring this machine in and get a new one.

M : Well, since you bought it so long ago, we can't replace it for you. Our store policy is that the item must be brought back within 30 days from the date of purchase. But you should contact the manufacturer. They'll probably replace it if it's still under warranty.

W : Oh, that's good, but I'm not sure where I put the paperwork. I'll have to go look for it.

M : In the meantime, I can forward your call to our customer service department. They might be able to tell you if the warranty is still in effect.

50. (　　) Why did the woman call the department store?
  (A) To complain about a defective product.
  (B) To inquire about an annual sale.
  (C) To apply for a job.
  (D) To schedule an appointment.

51. (　　) What does the man advise the woman to do?
  (A) Contact the manufacturer.
  (B) Purchase a new machine.
  (C) Go to the store's service desk.
  (D) Extend a warranty.

52. (　　) What will the man most likely do next?
  (A) Look up some information on his computer.
  (B) Issue a full refund for the machine.
  (C) Contact his supervisor.
  (D) Transfer the woman's call.

M : Hello, I'm planning to visit the Morganville Puppetry Museum and Workshop next week and I'm interested in seeing your craftsmen at work. Is that possible?

W : Certainly. Our craftsmen's workshop is open to visitors from 1:00 to 4:00 every afternoon. During that time, the puppet masters will be available to answer your questions about the facility and their work.

M : That sounds great. I have some friends who would be very interested as well.

W : That's fine but the workshop can't accommodate too many people. So if you have a big group, I suggest scheduling a private tour. However, there is an additional fee for that.

M : That's good to know. What is the additional fee?

W : Thirty dollars for any group over 10 people. The money goes directly toward the museum's numerous on-going projects.

53. (   ) What information does the man request?
    (A) Whether a facility is open to visitors.
    (B) Where the building is located.
    (C) Who will lead a tour.
    (D) How much tickets will cost.

54. (   ) What can visitors do at the workshop?
    (A) Observe a science experiment.
    (B) Buy some plants.
    (C) Watch a video about the laboratory's history.
    (D) Speak with some of the craftsmen.

55. (   ) What does the woman recommend?
    (A) Purchasing a ticket online.
    (B) Becoming a volunteer.
    (C) Booking a private tour.
    (D) Visiting on a weekend.

Questions 56 through 58 *refer to the following conversation.*

M : Tiffany, have you had a chance to try out the new software yet?

W : I've given it a look. I'll be using it starting next week to do payroll.

M : Well, I used it to calculate the total number of orders the warehouse can process in a given week. It has a lot of nice new features, but it doesn't run very fast. It took much longer than usual to run a report.

W : Hmm... The IT department is always asking for feedback. You should say something about that. Maybe there's something they can do to speed it up.

56. (   ) What will the woman use the new software for?
    (A) A Web design.
    (B) Sales figures.
    (C) Payroll.
    (D) Market research.

GO ON TO THE NEXT PAGE.

57. (　　) What is the problem with the software?
    (A) It does not produce required reports.
    (B) It runs very slowly.
    (C) It is difficult to install.
    (D) It is expensive.

58. (　　) What does the woman suggest?
    (A) Buying additional software.
    (B) Scheduling a training session.
    (C) Restarting a computer.
    (D) Contacting another department.

Questions 59 through 61 *refer to the following phone conversation.*

M : Hello, Dr. Taylor? This is Sam Pollard from the Omaha Medical Clinic's community outreach office. We're organizing a series of public lectures on the future of health care here on October 12. Would you be willing to speak at it?

W : I'd like to, but I'm not sure I'm available. We have a lot of interns starting at the hospital that week and I'll be mentoring a few of them. By the way, where are you holding the lectures?

M : The lectures will be held at the public library, which is just across the street from the clinic.

W : That's convenient enough.

M : OK... well... would you check your schedule and let me know when you're available? We'd really love to have you speak. We'd even be willing to reschedule the lecture if necessary.

59. (　　) What does the man ask the woman to do?
    (A) Coordinate an event.
    (B) Give a lecture.
    (C) Help a patient.
    (D) Chair a committee.

60. (　　) Why might Dr. Taylor be busy on October 12?
    (A) She will be going on leave.
    (B) She will be attending a board meeting.
    (C) She will be working with interns.
    (D) She will be performing surgery.

61. (　　) What does the man offer to do?
    (A) Arrange for transportation.
    (B) Speak to a manager.
    (C) Hire an assistant.
    (D) Reschedule an event.

W : Richard, after looking over the list of courses the Chadwick Institute is offering, there's one on public speaking I'd like to take. It will help me with my sales presentations. The company is still offering to pay for these types of professional development courses, aren't they?

M : I think so, Cassie, but you should ask someone in the personnel department. In the past, they have set aside some funding for training that's related to your job requirements. I'm sure they would approve it. But... how are you going to manage your job and taking a course like that?

W : True, I have been very busy lately. But since we finally signed with Wheel Works last week, I won't be putting in as much overtime in the foreseeable future. I'll tell you, I'm so relieved we finally closed that deal.

M : Me, too. It was a load off everybody's back. Say, doesn't Chadwick offer night courses?

W : Exactly. Which is why I'm confident I'll have time to take the course and do my job here at the firm.

62. (   ) What does the woman ask the man about?
  (A) Client interest in a product.
  (B) Requirements for a job promotion.
  (C) Adjustments to the work schedule.
  (D) Funding for professional development.

63. (   ) What does the woman say has recently happened at the company?
  (A) A management position was created.
  (B) An overtime policy was changed.
  (C) An agreement was reached with another company.
  (D) A retail location was closed.

64. (   ) Look at the graphic. Which course would the woman most likely take?
  (A) COM 102B.
  (B) COM 102C.
  (C) COM 102D.
  (D) COM 102E.

CHADWICK INSTITUTE OF PROFESSIONAL DEVELOPMENT

COLLEGE OF COMMUNICATIONS

Course	Code/Section	Instr.	Date/Time	
Public Speaking	COM102B	Baines, L.	MWF	0900-1100
Public Speaking	COM102C	Baines, L.	TTh	1300-1600
Public Speaking	COM102D	Garza, T.	MWF	1830-2030
Public Speaking	COM102E	Lupin, F.	Sat	0900-1530

GO ON TO THE NEXT PAGE.

W : My car is in the shop, so I'll need a rental starting tomorrow. Preferably something that gets good gas mileage.

M : We have plenty of vehicles available. How many days will you need the car?

W : //That's the thing.// I don't know for certain because it depends on how long it will take to repair mine. Three days, definitely, but I could end up needing it longer. Will that be a problem?

M : Not at all. I'll make a three-day reservation for now, but we can always extend that. Are you a member of our rewards program? There are lots of money-saving benefits and you get a discount on your next rental. If you haven't signed up yet, you can visit our Web site. It only takes a minute.

65. (   ) Where does the man most likely work?
    (A) At a car rental company.
    (B) At an auto repair shop.
    (C) At a hotel.
    (D) At a travel agency.

66. (   ) Why does the woman say, "That's the thing."?
    (A) She agrees with the man completely.
    (B) She has found the item she was looking for.
    (C) She will call back later.
    (D) She will explain her situation.

67. (   ) Look at the graphic. Which vehicle will the woman most likely select?
    (A) Ishii Courier.
    (B) Kramer Cruiser.
    (C) Taris Citicar Hybrid.
    (D) Cheon Blast Wagoneer Hybrid.

Belmonte Car Rental

CLASS
Economy Traveler Collection

Standard rate: $59.99 per day

Model*	Cap.	MPG
•Ishii Courier (or similar)	4+	43 or better
•Kramer Cruiser (or similar)	5+	36 or better
•Taris Citicar Hybrid	4+	57 or better
•Cheon Blast Wagoneer Hybrid	5-6+	46 or better

*Specific makes/models within a car class may vary in availability and features such as passenger seating, luggage capacity, equipment and mileage

W : Hi, this is Chloe Severin with Cuda Technologies here in Receda. I'm planning an employee mixer at a local bar, and I need a DJ for the event. Several of my associates recommended you and I'm wondering if you're available on Friday, July 9.

M : Um…yeah. Looks like I have nothing scheduled that evening. I don't have a lot of experience with corporate events, but I'm pleased your friends recommended me. How long will the event be?

W : We have the place to ourselves for three hours. It starts at 7:00, but if you could arrive around 6:30, that would be great.

M : No problem. Let me send you my standard contract for you to review and sign.

W : Great! I'll review the terms, and if you fit within my budget, I'll sign it and get it back to you ASAP. Most likely tomorrow morning.

68. (　　) What does the woman want to do?
    (A) Attend a training session.
    (B) Meet with a colleague.
    (C) Hire some entertainment.
    (D) Visit an art gallery.

69. (　　) What does the man say he will send?
    (A) His resume.
    (B) A contract.
    (C) Some references.
    (D) A mixtape.

70. (　　) Look at the graphic. Which of the following tasks has the woman completed?
    (A) She has posted a flyer in the employee break room.
    (B) She has hired the entertainment.
    (C) She has sent out an e-mail to her colleagues.
    (D) She has arranged for catering.

TO-DO LIST

Employee Mixer, Friday, July 9

☑ Get budget approved by Mr. Timmons

☑ Buy-out Jack's Cocktail Bar

☑ Arrange for catering (finger food; pizza, maybe?

☐ Hire DJ

☐ Pay deposit at Jack's

☐ Design and print flyer announcement

☐ Send out company-wide memo

GO ON TO THE NEXT PAGE.

PART 4

Questions 71 through 73 *refer to the following announcement.*

Welcome, Food Max shoppers. We're pleased to announce that Food Max now offers Food Max 2 Go——our new free home delivery service. Save time and effort by ordering products online and having them delivered right to your door——when you want them and when you need them. For complete details and to place your first order, visit our Web site, www.foodmax2go.com. Also, please be reminded that in preparation for the holiday tomorrow, Food Max will be closing at 6:00 p.m. this evening.

71. (　　) What new service is being announced?
    (A) Club membership.
    (B) Online banking.
    (C) Home delivery.
    (D) Catering.

72. (　　) What does the speaker suggest that listeners do?
    (A) Enter a contest.
    (B) Confirm an order.
    (C) Use a coupon.
    (D) Visit a website.

73. (　　) According to the speaker, what will happen this evening?
    (A) A business will close early.
    (B) A delivery will arrive.
    (C) A prizewinner will be announced.
    (D) A holiday sale will begin.

Questions 74 through 76 *refer to the following announcement.*

Last month, you guys made suggestions, and we listened. Therefore, I'm pleased to announce that Hartman Design has purchased a new Hexbot 3200 3-D printer. We'll now be able to manufacture our design models and prototypes right here in the office, which will increase our productivity. Now, the 3200 is the leading printer on the 3-D market and has some high-tech features. As a result, this Friday, we'll be holding two training sessions on how to use and maintain the unit——one in the morning, and one in the afternoon.

74. (   ) What is the purpose of the announcement?
    (A) To explain safety procedures.
    (B) To describe a new printer.
    (C) To share an employment opportunity.
    (D) To report an upcoming inspection.

75. (   ) What benefit does the speaker mention?
    (A) Reduced harm to the environment.
    (B) Greater flexibility with clients.
    (C) Increased worker productivity.
    (D) Fewer maintenance problems.

76. (   ) What will happen on Friday?
    (A) Some employees will be laid-off.
    (B) A printer will be delivered.
    (C) Clients will visit.
    (D) Training sessions will be held.

Questions 77 through 79 _refer to the following telephone message._

Hi, this message is for Deborah Parker. This is Ed Bowery from Bowery Brothers Plumbing. I was out last week to give you an estimate for replacing your copper piping with PVC. While I was there, you mentioned that you'd like the entire project to be completed by October 12. Well, after consulting with our master plumber, we can't guarantee it will be finished by the 12th. However, we would have the majority of the pipes replaced by that day. Please call me back and let me know if you'd like to discuss the project further. Thanks.

77. (   ) What project is the speaker discussing?
    (A) Building a garage.
    (B) Replacing some pipes.
    (C) Repairing a roof.
    (D) Remodeling a kitchen.

78. (   ) What problem does the speaker mention?
    (A) The weather will be poor.
    (B) A permit has been delayed.
    (C) A deadline cannot be met.
    (D) Some piping is not available.

GO ON TO THE NEXT PAGE.

79. (   ) What does the speaker offer to do?
    (A) Reduce a price.
    (B) Hire additional workers.
    (C) Refer other companies.
    (D) Discuss a project.

Questions 80 through 82 *refer to the following broadcast.*

And in tonight's WDBC-TV Tech Spotlight, telecommunications giant Votorola has recently announced that it will begin providing free wireless Internet to the public through thousands of wifi hotspots located in major metropolitan areas across the country. Internet access will not be limited to Votorola's customers but will be open to the public. The program is aimed at promoting digital literacy among the general population and will kick-off June 5 to coincide with the 102nd anniversary of Votorola's founding. Here to talk about the upcoming anniversary and free wireless initiative is Votorola company president Susan Sandberg.

80. (   ) What is Votorola planning to offer?
    (A) Research grants.
    (B) Software updates.
    (C) Internet access.
    (D) Summer internships.

81. (   ) Why did Votorola choose June 5 as a start date?
    (A) To respond to a client's request.
    (B) To meet a contract deadline.
    (C) To celebrate an anniversary.
    (D) To mark a holiday.

82. (   ) What will listeners most likely hear next?
    (A) A public service announcement.
    (B) An interview with a business executive.
    (C) Answers to audience questions.
    (D) More details about the new service.

Questions 83 through 85 *refer to the following announcement.*

And finally, the moment you've all been waiting for... It's my pleasure to announce the grand prize winner of the seventh annual Moko Motors Dream Car Design Contest, sponsored of course, by Moko Motors. We hope that drawing their dream cars lets the children not only have fun but also realize how vital their dreams are. We saw a lot of really creative designs this weekend, but //one dream car stood head and shoulders above the rest//. For his design of the ultra-lightweight glider car, the Road Bird, I would like to present this award to Robert Judd of Graysfield Elementary. Robert, come on up here and greet the audience!

83. (   ) What type of event is taking place?
    (A) A concert.
    (B) A grand opening.
    (C) A storewide sale.
    (D) An award ceremony.

84. (   ) What does the speaker mean by //"one car stood head and shoulders above the rest"//?
    (A) Its design was clearly superior to the others.
    (B) It is taller than all the other cars.
    (C) It resembles a human being.
    (D) It is the most reasonable of the entries.

85. (   ) What is implied about the contest?
    (A) It's for children.
    (B) It's never been held before.
    (C) It's sponsored by an elementary school.
    (D) It's held every other year.

Questions 86 through 88 refer to the following excerpt from a meeting.

Good morning, guys. Our first topic of discussion is the new building that we're designing for Johnson Corp. The client said that they want the architecture of the main headquarters to reflect their passion for innovation. So your assignment for the next few days is to come up with a building design concept that pushes the boundaries of design. I'll need your drafts on my desk no later than 5:00 p.m. Friday because I'm meeting with the client this weekend and they'll want to take a look at what we've come up with.

86. (   ) Where does the speaker most likely work?
    (A) At an advertising agency.
    (B) At a sporting goods store.
    (C) At an art gallery.
    (D) At an architectural firm.

GO ON TO THE NEXT PAGE.

87. (　　) What does the speaker ask the listeners to do?
    (A) Submit a design.
    (B) Organize some files.
    (C) Come to work early.
    (D) Contact a client.

88. (　　) According to the speaker, what will take place over the weekend?
    (A) A client meeting.
    (B) A community event.
    (C) A ground-breaking ceremony.
    (D) A professional workshop.

Questions 89 through 91 *refer to the following introduction.*

As the president of the Association of American Dentists, it's an honor to introduce Mr. Radim Letovsky. Mr. Letovsky comes to us with two decades of experience in the dental profession. He's just created a nationwide database that combines patient's dental records with other important information into one single program. This means that dental administration staff can better keep track of patient's dental history no matter where those patients received care in the past. So now, Mr. Letovsky will demonstrate how this program works and explain its various features.

89. (　　) What industry does Mr. Letovsky work in?
    (A) Architecture.
    (B) Health care.
    (C) Social media.
    (D) Finance.

90. (　　) What main accomplishment is Mr. Letovsky recognized for?
    (A) Starting a charitable organization.
    (B) Improving a training curriculum.
    (C) Publishing survey results.
    (D) Developing a national database.

91. (　　) According to the speaker, what will Mr. Letovsky do next?
    (A) Give a demonstration.
    (B) Tour a facility.
    (C) Talk to reporters.
    (D) Receive an award.

Good morning, and welcome to Mission Trail Regional Park. My name's Donna and I'll be guiding your hike today. Normally we'd be taking the Apache Trail to the Picnic and Camping Area, but the second part of that trail is closed for maintenance this week. So instead, we'll be starting out on the Apache Trail and changing over midway to the Cherokee Trail, as you can see here on the map. We'll break for our lunch at the end of the Cherokee Trail, and then we'll take the Oregon Trail back here to the Visitor's Center. Before we take off, let me remind you it's supposed to be sunny today; so it's a good idea to put on some sunscreen and wear a hat.

92. (   ) Who most likely are the listeners?
　　　　(A) Maintenance workers.
　　　　(B) Bus drivers.
　　　　(C) Tourists.
　　　　(D) Park rangers.

93. (   ) Look at the graphic. Where will the listeners be unable to go today?
　　　　(A) Lake Opal.
　　　　(B) Swan Garden.
　　　　(C) The Picnic and Camping Area.
　　　　(D) The Visitor's Center.

94. (   ) What does the woman encourage the listeners to do?
　　　　(A) Bring a map.
　　　　(B) Check the weather forecast.
　　　　(C) Store their belongings.
　　　　(D) Use sun protection.

GO ON TO THE NEXT PAGE.

Hi, Mr. Lambert. This is Gretchen from Horizons Travel Agency, calling to confirm your upcoming trip to Argentina. Also, the last time you were in the office, we discussed some of the preparations you need to make for your trip, and I apologize for not mentioning this before. If you're planning to use your mobile phone during the trip, you'll want to purchase a different SIM card. Our SIM cards are not compatible with the networks in Argentina. There are several different Web sites that offer international phone cards—I recommend SA Mobile dot com. Anyway, I just emailed your flight itinerary. Feel free to contact me with any questions.

95. (   ) What type of business does the speaker work for?
  (A) A bookstore.
  (B) A mobile phone carrier.
  (C) An electronics store.
  (D) A travel agency.

96. (   ) What does the speaker advise the listener to purchase?
  (A) A different SIM card.
  (B) A new computer.
  (C) An insurance policy.
  (D) An economy plane ticket.

97. (   ) Look at the graphic. What did the speaker send Mr. Lambert?
  (A) A list of recommendations.
  (B) A guidebook.
  (C) A flight schedule.
  (D) A pricing brochure.

Itinerary Receipt	**SILVER SKY AIRLINES**

Booking Details:
CONFIRMED
Booking Date:
May 13

Booking Reference Number:
BVT90L9

(00) 0 0123456 000000001 8

Guest Details
Lambert, Todd

Route	Flight #	Departure	Arrival
Chicago - Buenos Aires	SS870	June 12, 22:00	June 13, 12:00
Buenos Aires - Chicago	SS871	June 24, 15:00	June 25, 05:00

Good afternoon, this is Maryanne Walters calling from Jensen and Parker Associates. I wanted to follow up with you about the catering order form that I e-mailed you last week. It's for our company's board meeting tomorrow. I'd like to double the number of beverages. People might get extra thirsty during such a long meeting. Also, I wanted to let you know that when you arrive at our headquarters, you'll have to check in at the security desk to pick up a visitor's badge. I've already let the security guard know, so there should be a badge ready for you.

98. (   )   What type of event is being catered?
(A) A product launch.
(B) A business meeting.
(C) An academic lecture.
(D) A retirement party.

99. (   )   Look at the graphic. Which quantity on the original order form is no longer accurate?
(A) 2.
(B) 3.
(C) 20.
(D) 24.

CATERING ORDER FORM		
Qty.	Item	Price
2	Fruit trays	2@15.00=30.00
3	Deli platters	2@25.00=50.00
24	Assorted pastries	24@1.50=36.00
20	Bottled water (16 oz.)	20@1.00=20.00
20	Soft drinks (12 oz. can)	20@0.75=15.00
		Total: 151.00

100. (   )   What is the listener asked to do tomorrow?
(A) Arrive early to set up a room.
(B) Bring additional staff.
(C) Pick up an identification badge.
(D) Give a speech.

GO ON TO THE NEXT PAGE.

NO TEST MATERIAL ON THIS PAGE

New TOEIC Speaking Test

Question 1: Read a Text Aloud

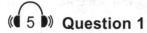 **Question 1**

Directions: In this part of the test, you will read aloud the text on the screen. You will have 45 seconds to prepare. Then you will have 45 seconds to read the text aloud.

Whether a high-speed rail system ever gets built in the United States is still up in the air, but if it does, artist and activist Alfred Wu has figured out exactly where those speedy rail lines should go. Wu started working on this map in 2009, when President Obama's plan to build a high-speed rail system was unveiled.

PREPARATION TIME
00 : 00 : 45

RESPONSE TIME
00 : 00 : 45

GO ON TO THE NEXT PAGE.

Question 2: Read a Text Aloud

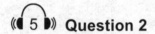 **Question 2**

Directions: In this part of the test, you will read aloud the text on the screen. You will have 45 seconds to prepare. Then you will have 45 seconds to read the text aloud.

Thank you for scheduling your recent credit card payment online. Your payment in the amount of $100.00 will be posted to your account ending in 9226 April 7, 2017. If you have questions, please call the Customer Service number on the back of your credit card. Thanks again for using online payments.

PREPARATION TIME
00 : 00 : 45

RESPONSE TIME
00 : 00 : 45

Question 3: Describe a Picture

 **Question 3**

Directions: In this part of the test, you will describe the picture on your screen in as much detail as you can. You will have 30 seconds to prepare your response. Then you will have 45 seconds to speak about the picture.

PREPARATION TIME
00 : 00 : 30

RESPONSE TIME
00 : 00 : 45

GO ON TO THE NEXT PAGE.

Question 3: Describe a Picture

答題範例

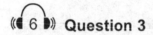 **Question 3**

This is a picture of Paris at night.

Paris is one of the world's most recognizable cities.

It is the number one tourist destination on the planet.

The focus of the picture is the Eiffel Tower.

It is an iconic landmark.

Like Paris, everybody knows what it is when they see it.

The tower is brightly lit.

It's a beautiful sight.

I'm sure thousands of tourists were there at the time the photo
    was taken.

There's a waning moon in the sky.

It hangs just to the left of the Eiffel Tower.

What a lovely night!

The plaza of the Tower is also lit up.

There is a series of fountains in the foreground.

The River Seine flows between sections of the plaza.

In the distance you can see the rest of Paris.

It's really a fantastic city.

They don't have many skyscrapers in Paris.

Questions 4-6: Respond to Questions

 **Question 4**

Directions: In this part of the test, you will answer three questions. For each question, begin responding immediately after you hear a beep. No preparation time is provided. You will have 15 seconds to respond to Questions 4 and 5 and 30 seconds to respond to Question 6.

Imagine that you are participating in a research study about relationships. You have agreed to answer some questions in a telephone interview.

Question 4
Are you currently in a relationship?

Question 5
How long was the longest relationship you've ever had?

Question 6
What level of commitment is or was involved in your relationship?

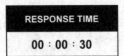

GO ON TO THE NEXT PAGE.

Questions 4-6: Respond to Questions

答題範例

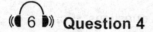 **Question 4**

Are you currently in a relationship?

Answer

> Yes, I am.
>
> I am married.
>
> My wife's name is Janice.

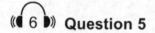 **Question 5**

How long was the longest relationship you've ever had?

Answer

> Five years.
>
> It was before I met my wife.
>
> We've been married for three years.

Questions 4-6: Respond to Questions

 **Question 6**

What level of commitment is or was involved in your relationship?

Answer

> Well, we're married.
>
> So that means total commitment.
>
> That's what marriage means.
>
>
> Plus, we have a kid.
>
> Therefore, I would say that our level of commitment is
>
>   even higher than that of childless couples.
>
> Our family comes first.
>
>
> Although I am committed to my family, I still have other
>
>   interests.
>
> I hang out with friends on occasion.
>
> And I'm really into music.

GO ON TO THE NEXT PAGE.

Questions 7-9: Respond to Questions Using Information Provided

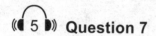 **Question 7**

Directions: In this part of the test, you will answer three questions based on the information provided. You will have 30 seconds to read the information before the questions begin. For each question, begin responding immediately after you hear a beep. No additional preparation time is provided. You will have 15 seconds to respond to Questions 7 and 8 and 30 seconds to respond to Question 9.

ATTENTION GREATER INDIANAPOLIS HOME AND BUSINESS OWNERS!

How long would you frequent a restaurant after learning they only clean the rims of the glasses customers drink out of? Disgusting, right? Well, why accept this type of service from a cleaning service——a place that only spot cleans? Well, with Clean Arlene you can expect a lot more ——expect to receive the type of cleaning for your home or business that can only be described as "meticulous." Clean Arlene has over 20 years of experience in cleaning perfection. This rings true due to the fact that many customers have trusted Clean Arlene for years. And when you see repeat business like this, you know something is being done right! Pick up the phone and find out for yourself—595-9199. When it comes to cleaning a residence or business, you can be sure that Clean Arlene will be consistent, on time, and ready to take on any challenge. Call Clean Arlene today 595-9199. Clean Arlene is bonded, insured, and backed by stellar references!

Hello! This is Rocky. I'm calling about Clean Arlene. Would you mind if I asked a few questions?

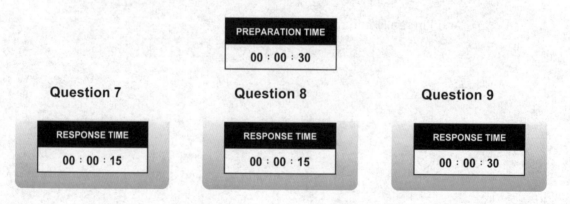

PREPARATION TIME
00 : 00 : 30

Question 7

RESPONSE TIME
00 : 00 : 15

Question 8

RESPONSE TIME
00 : 00 : 15

Question 9

RESPONSE TIME
00 : 00 : 30

Questions 7-9: Respond to Questions Using Information Provided

答題範例

 **Question 7**

How long has Clean Arlene been in business?

Answer

> We've been in business over 20 years.
>
> Most of our customers have been with us for over 10
>
> years.
>
> Thus, the majority of our business comes from repeat
>
> customers.

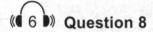 **Question 8**

What will Clean Arlene clean?

Answer

> If it needs cleaning, we'll do it.
>
> Most of our clients are homeowners.
>
> We also clean a few local businesses.

GO ON TO THE NEXT PAGE.

Questions 7-9: Respond to Questions Using Information Provided

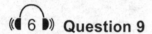 **Question 9**

What can I expect from Clean Arlene's service?

Answer

You can expect to receive the type of cleaning for your

home or business that can only be described as

"meticulous."

Clean Arlene demands cleaning perfection.

Many customers have trusted Clean Arlene for years.

And when you see repeat business like this, you know

something is being done right!

You can be sure that Clean Arlene will be consistent.

We will be on time; we will be ready to take on any

challenge.

Cleaning is our passion.

We're not just good at it—we live to do it.

And finally, Clean Arlene is bonded, insured, and backed

by stellar references!

Question 10: Propose a Solution

 **Question 10**

Directions: In this part of the test, you will be presented with a problem and asked to propose a solution. You will have 30 seconds to prepare. Then you will have 60 seconds to speak. In your response, be sure to show that you recognize the problem, and propose a way of dealing with the problem.

In your response, be sure to

- show that you recognize the caller's problem, and
- propose a way of dealing with the problem.

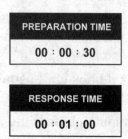

PREPARATION TIME
00 : 00 : 30

RESPONSE TIME
00 : 01 : 00

GO ON TO THE NEXT PAGE.

Question 10: Propose a Solution

答題範例

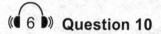 **Question 10**

Voice Message

I have a 2001 Buick Regal with about 140,000 miles on it. Lately I've had problems with it stalling while driving, occasionally when accelerating but mainly when idling. If it happens while I'm driving I can give it a little bit of gas and it won't stall, but I can't do anything if it stalls while I'm idling. Also, when I try to crank it back up, I usually have to let it sit for about five minutes before the engine turns. But it's like it's not getting any gas. Any ideas as to what is causing this?

Question 10: Propose a Solution

答題範例

Hi, this is Jeff with Condor Auto Solutions.

I understand you are having a problem with your car stalling.

You could schedule an appointment to have it looked at.

Or I could suggest a few things before doing that.

Every engine requires spark, fuel, and compression to run.

That's what we have to look for.

These are the basics that need to be tested and isolate a cause.

First, test your spark plugs using a spark tester.

If you don't get a spark, check the power supply on the positive
  terminal of the coil.

If the power supply is good, you need new spark plugs.

Next, open up the carburetor.

You shouldn't see any fuel remaining in the float bowl.

If you do, that means you're flooded——getting too much fuel.

Adjust the choke to reduce the flow of fuel.

Finally, if the spark plugs and carburetor look good, it's probably the
  fuel injector itself.

Sometimes they go bad and need to be replaced.

It's a common issue with the 2001 Regal.

I hope I've been able to solve your problem.

If you need more assistance, please bring the car in.

Of course, you can always call me at 343-0099.

GO ON TO THE NEXT PAGE.

Question 11: Express an Opinion

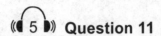 **Question 11**

Directions: In this part of the test, you will give your opinion about a specific topic. Be sure to say as much as you can in the time allowed. You will have 15 seconds to prepare. Then you will have 60 seconds to speak.

Do you think space exploration is necessary for the survival of mankind? Give reasons to support your opinion.

PREPARATION TIME
00 : 00 : 15

RESPONSE TIME
00 : 01 : 00

Question 11: Express an Opinion

答題範例

 **Question 11**

Yes, I do. I think it is part of our nature as human beings that we want to explore.
We have a natural desire to understand the world in which we live.
Space exploration is the logical extension of that need.

Exploration is important because it provides us with an opportunity to make
  advancements in science and technology.
These can be a benefit to all of humankind, such as in the areas of communications and
  remote sensing.
Therefore, space technology has become an integral part of our daily lives.

Cellular technology, for example, is dependent on satellite communications.
Satellites are also used to monitor changes in Earth's climate and ocean circulation, for
  weather forecasting, in aviation and marine navigation, and for military reconnaissance.
The space program also provides an opportunity for nations to work together.

Many governments are currently involved in the development of space technology.
In the near future, other nations will be added to this list.
It is vital to our national interest that the United States remain the leader in developing
  new space technologies; this will insure the peaceful exploration of space by all.

When Christopher Columbus wanted to sail west, at the time, it was considered a fool's
  errand.
Eventually people realized that Columbus had transformed the course of human history.
Space exploration is similar, inasmuch as some people think it's futile.

It may only be in the future that people appreciate what a huge impact it's had on society.
Who knows what incredible discoveries are just around the corner?
Who knows what revolutionary new technologies may appear as a result of space
  exploration?

GO ON TO THE NEXT PAGE.

NO TEST MATERIAL ON THIS PAGE

New TOEIC Writing Test

Questions 1-5: Write a Sentence Based on a Picture

Question 1

Directions: Write ONE sentence based on the picture using the TWO words or phrases under it. You may change the forms of the words and you may use them in any order.

girl / window

GO ON TO THE NEXT PAGE.

Questions 1-5: Write a Sentence Based on a Picture

Question 2

Directions: Write ONE sentence based on the picture using the TWO words or phrases under it. You may change the forms of the words and you may use them in any order.

spectators / fireworks

Questions 1-5: Write a Sentence Based on a Picture

Question 3

Directions: Write ONE sentence based on the picture using the TWO words or phrases under it. You may change the forms of the words and you may use them in any order.

swim / lane

GO ON TO THE NEXT PAGE.

Questions 1-5: Write a Sentence Based on a Picture

Question 4

Directions: Write ONE sentence based on the picture using the TWO words or phrases under it. You may change the forms of the words and you may use them in any order.

cargo / ocean

Questions 1-5: Write a Sentence Based on a Picture

Question 5

Directions: Write ONE sentence based on the picture using the TWO words or phrases under it. You may change the forms of the words and you may use them in any order.

students / books

GO ON TO THE NEXT PAGE.

Questions 6-7: Respond to a written request

Question 6

Directions: Read the e-mail below.

From:	Ron Rush
Sent:	Tuesday, March 17
To:	All staff

Hey guys, please let me know if you are planning to submit a vacation request in April. Open slots are going fast, so get back to me ASAP.

Thanks,
Ron

Directions: Reply to Ron as an employee of the company. You don't want to submit a vacation request for April, but are curious about availability in May.

Questions 6-7: Respond to a written request

答題範例

Question 6

Ron,

In response to your email, I'm not submitting a request for April, but I'm thinking about taking two weeks off in May. How is the month shaping up in terms of availability? I'm wondering if I should submit the request now. Any feedback will be much appreciated.

Thanks,
Sally

GO ON TO THE NEXT PAGE.

Questions 6-7: Respond to a written request

Question 7

Directions: Read the e-mail below.

From:	Jimmy Carl Black
Sent:	Sunday, January 6
To:	Ahmet Zappa
Subject:	Studio

Ahmet,

I was wondering if it would be possible to book some

studio time during the first two weeks of October. I'd

love to record at your place.

Yours,

JCB

Directions: Reply as Ahmet and deny Jimmie Carl Black's request.
Give one reason why.

Questions 6-7: Respond to a written request

答題範例

Question 7

JCB,

Great to hear from you, man! I was just thinking about you the other day. I hope you're well. However, unfortunately, the studio was booked for the entire month of October by Jay-Z. He's requested a complete lockout, so I have no flexibility on my end. Perhaps you'd consider changing your dates? Let me know.

Ahmet

GO ON TO THE NEXT PAGE.

Questions 8: Write an opinion essay

Question 8

Directions: Read the question below. You have 30 minutes to plan, write, and revise your essay. Typically, an effective response will contain a minimum of 300 words.

It's been said that the only sure things in life are "death and taxes." Can you think of any other inevitable events in your life?

Questions 8: Write an opinion essay

答題範例

Question 8

I believe that feeling that life isn't fair is also inevitable in life. At some point, I believe that life seems unfair because most of the time you don't get the things that you want, or because sometimes things don't go the way you want them to.

When I was five years old, my dad was diagnosed with kidney failure. He was put on a transplant list and immediately began dialysis. Growing up with an ill father most of my life, I learned a lot about kidneys, dialysis, and diabetes, which my father also had. The combination of kidney failure on top of my father's type 2 diabetes weakened his immune system greatly.

He was on the transplant list for seven years before he got the call when I was twelve years old. I remember being so happy for him I cried out of excitement. The drive to the hospital seemed so long, but before I knew it he was already in surgery. The surgery seemed to be twice as long as it really was, but when it was over, everything had gone well. With tears of joy came my tears of worry. I knew just how serious this surgery was and I was very concerned. Many people are very lucky when they receive a transplant, and their body takes to the new organ. My father did not have the same luck. My father's body rejected the kidney. He became very sick and passed away when I was just fourteen.

Usually it is the little things that make us believe that life just isn't fair. When my father passed away, it completely changed my perspective on life. Instead of dwelling on how life isn't fair, I learned to love and appreciate the loved ones I have, while they're here. Life is unpredictable and unexpected, but that's the beauty of it.

There are a lot of things that I think of now that I wish I had done with my dad. I try not to focus on what we missed out on and instead focus on the great times we did have together. Losing a loved one at such a young age can have a huge effect on your life. Some people deal with death in a negative way, while others may use it as a way to change who they are. I am not as selfish as I used to be, and I try not to take anything I have for granted. I feel I am lucky enough just to be a healthy, happy person.

TOEIC ANSWER SHEET

READING SECTION

No.	ANSWER	No.	ANSWER	No.	ANSWER	No.	ANSWER	No.	ANSWER
Part 5	A B C D		A B C D		A B C D	**Part 6**	A B C D	**Part 7**	A B C D
101	Ⓐ Ⓑ Ⓒ Ⓓ	111	Ⓐ Ⓑ Ⓒ Ⓓ	121	Ⓐ Ⓑ Ⓒ Ⓓ	131	Ⓐ Ⓑ Ⓒ Ⓓ	141	Ⓐ Ⓑ Ⓒ Ⓓ
102	Ⓐ Ⓑ Ⓒ Ⓓ	112	Ⓐ Ⓑ Ⓒ Ⓓ	122	Ⓐ Ⓑ Ⓒ Ⓓ	132	Ⓐ Ⓑ Ⓒ Ⓓ	142	Ⓐ Ⓑ Ⓒ Ⓓ
103	Ⓐ Ⓑ Ⓒ Ⓓ	113	Ⓐ Ⓑ Ⓒ Ⓓ	123	Ⓐ Ⓑ Ⓒ Ⓓ	133	Ⓐ Ⓑ Ⓒ Ⓓ	143	Ⓐ Ⓑ Ⓒ Ⓓ
104	Ⓐ Ⓑ Ⓒ Ⓓ	114	Ⓐ Ⓑ Ⓒ Ⓓ	124	Ⓐ Ⓑ Ⓒ Ⓓ	134	Ⓐ Ⓑ Ⓒ Ⓓ	144	Ⓐ Ⓑ Ⓒ Ⓓ
105	Ⓐ Ⓑ Ⓒ Ⓓ	115	Ⓐ Ⓑ Ⓒ Ⓓ	125	Ⓐ Ⓑ Ⓒ Ⓓ	135	Ⓐ Ⓑ Ⓒ Ⓓ	145	Ⓐ Ⓑ Ⓒ Ⓓ
106	Ⓐ Ⓑ Ⓒ Ⓓ	116	Ⓐ Ⓑ Ⓒ Ⓓ	126	Ⓐ Ⓑ Ⓒ Ⓓ	136	Ⓐ Ⓑ Ⓒ Ⓓ	146	Ⓐ Ⓑ Ⓒ Ⓓ
107	Ⓐ Ⓑ Ⓒ Ⓓ	117	Ⓐ Ⓑ Ⓒ Ⓓ	127	Ⓐ Ⓑ Ⓒ Ⓓ	137	Ⓐ Ⓑ Ⓒ Ⓓ	147	Ⓐ Ⓑ Ⓒ Ⓓ
108	Ⓐ Ⓑ Ⓒ Ⓓ	118	Ⓐ Ⓑ Ⓒ Ⓓ	128	Ⓐ Ⓑ Ⓒ Ⓓ	138	Ⓐ Ⓑ Ⓒ Ⓓ	148	Ⓐ Ⓑ Ⓒ Ⓓ
109	Ⓐ Ⓑ Ⓒ Ⓓ	119	Ⓐ Ⓑ Ⓒ Ⓓ	129	Ⓐ Ⓑ Ⓒ Ⓓ	139	Ⓐ Ⓑ Ⓒ Ⓓ	149	Ⓐ Ⓑ Ⓒ Ⓓ
110	Ⓐ Ⓑ Ⓒ Ⓓ	120	Ⓐ Ⓑ Ⓒ Ⓓ	130	Ⓐ Ⓑ Ⓒ Ⓓ	140	Ⓐ Ⓑ Ⓒ Ⓓ	150	Ⓐ Ⓑ Ⓒ Ⓓ

No.	ANSWER	No.	ANSWER	No.	ANSWER	No.	ANSWER	No.	ANSWER
	A B C D		A B C D		A B C D		A B C D		A B C D
151	Ⓐ Ⓑ Ⓒ Ⓓ	161	Ⓐ Ⓑ Ⓒ Ⓓ	171	Ⓐ Ⓑ Ⓒ Ⓓ	181	Ⓐ Ⓑ Ⓒ Ⓓ	191	Ⓐ Ⓑ Ⓒ Ⓓ
152	Ⓐ Ⓑ Ⓒ Ⓓ	162	Ⓐ Ⓑ Ⓒ Ⓓ	172	Ⓐ Ⓑ Ⓒ Ⓓ	182	Ⓐ Ⓑ Ⓒ Ⓓ	192	Ⓐ Ⓑ Ⓒ Ⓓ
153	Ⓐ Ⓑ Ⓒ Ⓓ	163	Ⓐ Ⓑ Ⓒ Ⓓ	173	Ⓐ Ⓑ Ⓒ Ⓓ	183	Ⓐ Ⓑ Ⓒ Ⓓ	193	Ⓐ Ⓑ Ⓒ Ⓓ
154	Ⓐ Ⓑ Ⓒ Ⓓ	164	Ⓐ Ⓑ Ⓒ Ⓓ	174	Ⓐ Ⓑ Ⓒ Ⓓ	184	Ⓐ Ⓑ Ⓒ Ⓓ	194	Ⓐ Ⓑ Ⓒ Ⓓ
155	Ⓐ Ⓑ Ⓒ Ⓓ	165	Ⓐ Ⓑ Ⓒ Ⓓ	175	Ⓐ Ⓑ Ⓒ Ⓓ	185	Ⓐ Ⓑ Ⓒ Ⓓ	195	Ⓐ Ⓑ Ⓒ Ⓓ
156	Ⓐ Ⓑ Ⓒ Ⓓ	166	Ⓐ Ⓑ Ⓒ Ⓓ	176	Ⓐ Ⓑ Ⓒ Ⓓ	186	Ⓐ Ⓑ Ⓒ Ⓓ	196	Ⓐ Ⓑ Ⓒ Ⓓ
157	Ⓐ Ⓑ Ⓒ Ⓓ	167	Ⓐ Ⓑ Ⓒ Ⓓ	177	Ⓐ Ⓑ Ⓒ Ⓓ	187	Ⓐ Ⓑ Ⓒ Ⓓ	197	Ⓐ Ⓑ Ⓒ Ⓓ
158	Ⓐ Ⓑ Ⓒ Ⓓ	168	Ⓐ Ⓑ Ⓒ Ⓓ	178	Ⓐ Ⓑ Ⓒ Ⓓ	188	Ⓐ Ⓑ Ⓒ Ⓓ	198	Ⓐ Ⓑ Ⓒ Ⓓ
159	Ⓐ Ⓑ Ⓒ Ⓓ	169	Ⓐ Ⓑ Ⓒ Ⓓ	179	Ⓐ Ⓑ Ⓒ Ⓓ	189	Ⓐ Ⓑ Ⓒ Ⓓ	199	Ⓐ Ⓑ Ⓒ Ⓓ
160	Ⓐ Ⓑ Ⓒ Ⓓ	170	Ⓐ Ⓑ Ⓒ Ⓓ	180	Ⓐ Ⓑ Ⓒ Ⓓ	190	Ⓐ Ⓑ Ⓒ Ⓓ	200	Ⓐ Ⓑ Ⓒ Ⓓ

LISTENING SECTION

No.	ANSWER	No.	ANSWER	No.	ANSWER	No.	ANSWER
Part 1	A B C D	**Part 2**	A B C D	**Part 3**	A B C D	**Part 4**	A B C D
1	Ⓐ Ⓑ Ⓒ Ⓓ	11	Ⓐ Ⓑ Ⓒ	41	Ⓐ Ⓑ Ⓒ Ⓓ	71	Ⓐ Ⓑ Ⓒ Ⓓ
2	Ⓐ Ⓑ Ⓒ Ⓓ	12	Ⓐ Ⓑ Ⓒ	42	Ⓐ Ⓑ Ⓒ Ⓓ	72	Ⓐ Ⓑ Ⓒ Ⓓ
3	Ⓐ Ⓑ Ⓒ Ⓓ	13	Ⓐ Ⓑ Ⓒ	43	Ⓐ Ⓑ Ⓒ Ⓓ	73	Ⓐ Ⓑ Ⓒ Ⓓ
4	Ⓐ Ⓑ Ⓒ Ⓓ	14	Ⓐ Ⓑ Ⓒ	44	Ⓐ Ⓑ Ⓒ Ⓓ	74	Ⓐ Ⓑ Ⓒ Ⓓ
5	Ⓐ Ⓑ Ⓒ	15	Ⓐ Ⓑ Ⓒ	45	Ⓐ Ⓑ Ⓒ Ⓓ	75	Ⓐ Ⓑ Ⓒ Ⓓ
6	Ⓐ Ⓑ Ⓒ	16	Ⓐ Ⓑ Ⓒ	46	Ⓐ Ⓑ Ⓒ Ⓓ	76	Ⓐ Ⓑ Ⓒ Ⓓ
7	Ⓐ Ⓑ Ⓒ	17	Ⓐ Ⓑ Ⓒ	47	Ⓐ Ⓑ Ⓒ Ⓓ	77	Ⓐ Ⓑ Ⓒ Ⓓ
8	Ⓐ Ⓑ Ⓒ	18	Ⓐ Ⓑ Ⓒ	48	Ⓐ Ⓑ Ⓒ Ⓓ	78	Ⓐ Ⓑ Ⓒ Ⓓ
9	Ⓐ Ⓑ Ⓒ	19	Ⓐ Ⓑ Ⓒ	49	Ⓐ Ⓑ Ⓒ Ⓓ	79	Ⓐ Ⓑ Ⓒ Ⓓ
10	Ⓐ Ⓑ Ⓒ	20	Ⓐ Ⓑ Ⓒ	50	Ⓐ Ⓑ Ⓒ Ⓓ	80	Ⓐ Ⓑ Ⓒ Ⓓ

No.	ANSWER	No.	ANSWER	No.	ANSWER	No.	ANSWER
	A B C D		A B C D		A B C D		A B C D
21	Ⓐ Ⓑ Ⓒ	31	Ⓐ Ⓑ Ⓒ Ⓓ	51	Ⓐ Ⓑ Ⓒ Ⓓ	81	Ⓐ Ⓑ Ⓒ Ⓓ
22	Ⓐ Ⓑ Ⓒ	32	Ⓐ Ⓑ Ⓒ Ⓓ	52	Ⓐ Ⓑ Ⓒ Ⓓ	82	Ⓐ Ⓑ Ⓒ Ⓓ
23	Ⓐ Ⓑ Ⓒ	33	Ⓐ Ⓑ Ⓒ Ⓓ	53	Ⓐ Ⓑ Ⓒ Ⓓ	83	Ⓐ Ⓑ Ⓒ Ⓓ
24	Ⓐ Ⓑ Ⓒ	34	Ⓐ Ⓑ Ⓒ Ⓓ	54	Ⓐ Ⓑ Ⓒ Ⓓ	84	Ⓐ Ⓑ Ⓒ Ⓓ
25	Ⓐ Ⓑ Ⓒ	35	Ⓐ Ⓑ Ⓒ Ⓓ	55	Ⓐ Ⓑ Ⓒ Ⓓ	85	Ⓐ Ⓑ Ⓒ Ⓓ
26	Ⓐ Ⓑ Ⓒ	36	Ⓐ Ⓑ Ⓒ Ⓓ	56	Ⓐ Ⓑ Ⓒ Ⓓ	86	Ⓐ Ⓑ Ⓒ Ⓓ
27	Ⓐ Ⓑ Ⓒ	37	Ⓐ Ⓑ Ⓒ Ⓓ	57	Ⓐ Ⓑ Ⓒ Ⓓ	87	Ⓐ Ⓑ Ⓒ Ⓓ
28	Ⓐ Ⓑ Ⓒ	38	Ⓐ Ⓑ Ⓒ Ⓓ	58	Ⓐ Ⓑ Ⓒ Ⓓ	88	Ⓐ Ⓑ Ⓒ Ⓓ
29	Ⓐ Ⓑ Ⓒ	39	Ⓐ Ⓑ Ⓒ Ⓓ	59	Ⓐ Ⓑ Ⓒ Ⓓ	89	Ⓐ Ⓑ Ⓒ Ⓓ
30	Ⓐ Ⓑ Ⓒ	40	Ⓐ Ⓑ Ⓒ Ⓓ	60	Ⓐ Ⓑ Ⓒ Ⓓ	90	Ⓐ Ⓑ Ⓒ Ⓓ

No.	ANSWER	No.	ANSWER
	A B C D		A B C D
61	Ⓐ Ⓑ Ⓒ Ⓓ	91	Ⓐ Ⓑ Ⓒ Ⓓ
62	Ⓐ Ⓑ Ⓒ Ⓓ	92	Ⓐ Ⓑ Ⓒ Ⓓ
63	Ⓐ Ⓑ Ⓒ Ⓓ	93	Ⓐ Ⓑ Ⓒ Ⓓ
64	Ⓐ Ⓑ Ⓒ Ⓓ	94	Ⓐ Ⓑ Ⓒ Ⓓ
65	Ⓐ Ⓑ Ⓒ Ⓓ	95	Ⓐ Ⓑ Ⓒ Ⓓ
66	Ⓐ Ⓑ Ⓒ Ⓓ	96	Ⓐ Ⓑ Ⓒ Ⓓ
67	Ⓐ Ⓑ Ⓒ Ⓓ	97	Ⓐ Ⓑ Ⓒ Ⓓ
68	Ⓐ Ⓑ Ⓒ Ⓓ	98	Ⓐ Ⓑ Ⓒ Ⓓ
69	Ⓐ Ⓑ Ⓒ Ⓓ	99	Ⓐ Ⓑ Ⓒ Ⓓ
70	Ⓐ Ⓑ Ⓒ Ⓓ	100	Ⓐ Ⓑ Ⓒ Ⓓ

REGISTRATION No.

姓 名

NAME

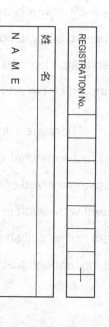